HOME AND AWAY

DAVE BIDINI

HOME
AND
AWAY

One Writer's Inspiring Experience at

The Homeless World Cup

Skyhorse Publishing

Skyhorse Publishing books may be purchased in bulk at special discounts
for sales promotion, corporate gifts, fund-raising, or educational
purposes. Special editions can also be created to specifications. For
details, contact the Special Sales Department, Skyhorse Publishing,
307 West 36th Street, 11th Floor, New York, NY 10018 or
info@skyhorsepublishing.com.

Skyhorse® and Skyhorse Publishing® are registered trademarks of
Skyhorse Publishing, Inc.®, a Delaware corporation.

www.skyhorsepublishing.com

Originally published in Canada by Greystone Books, an imprint of Douglas &
McIntyre Publishers, Inc., 2010

First Skyhorse edition, 2011

10 9 8 7 6 5 4 3 2 1

Library of Congress Cataloging-in-Publication Data is available on file.
ISBN: 978-1-61608-306-9

Printed in the United States of America

For PQ

CONTENTS

ACKNOWLEDGEMENTS

THE AUTHOR WISHES to acknowledge editor Mark Weinstein of Skyhorse, who, a few years ago, wrote an email to say: "I think I have your next book." Also, thank you to everyone from Street Soccer Canada and to Rick McDonald: among the finest men.

Considering the sensitive nature of this book, some names have been changed and certain details masked. Otherwise, this story has remained true to real events.

"Here am I,
  ready as I will ever be.
  Feeling equal parts of
  lonely
  and just being free."

BOB SNIDER
"If I Sang It Pretty"

HOME AND AWAY

SHADOW

AND

MUSCLE

I N THE BIG city where I live—Toronto, which
has been my home for my entire life—there
are 16,000 homeless people living among us. The shelters
are stuffed with bodies, and, every winter, dozens of men and
women are found dead on the streets. The decline in mental
health services and the clawing away of the jobless safety net
by successive government regimes has made it harder for people to find their way back after falling through the economic
cracks. According to the City of Toronto's annual homeless report, half a million Toronto households have incomes
below the poverty line; a quarter of a million pay more than
30 percent of their income on rent; 71,000 families are on the
city's waiting list for affordable social housing; and 32,000
citizens (including 6,500 children) stayed in a shelter at least
one night over the past year. These numbers, however, suffer

from the nature of their subject. Accurately counting homeless people is a little like chasing ghosts, and the number is
almost always higher, considering the depth of the shadows
they are forced to occupy.

Despite the pervasiveness of the homeless, many of
us—myself included—pass them as if moving through the
shadow of a cloud. Slumped against the sides of buildings,
surrounded by shopping bags at the end of a bench in a frozen bus shelter, or curled in the fetal position under the glare
of a bank kiosk's lights, they may become for us almost like
pigeons: you throw them a crumb every now and then and
watch their reaction out of the corner of your eye while you
keep moving. Interaction is limited, but occasionally, lives
intersect.

One afternoon, while riding her bike, my wife happened
across a fallen man hanging halfway into traffic over the
curbside. She stopped and asked if he was okay and if he
might want to take himself out of the way of traffic for fear
of being run over. He roused himself long enough to pull his
body to safety. She started to pedal away, but the man raised
his head and said: "Hold on, wait." Janet turned back. He
rubbed his face for a moment, then asked her: "So, how are
you doing?"

Homelessness and poverty aren't limited to my town, and
to yours. While putting this book together, I opened the front
section of the September 12, 2009, edition of the *International
Herald Tribune* and, as an experiment, tried looking for stories in which these issues were the focus. It hadn't seemed
like a particularly distressing week; yet the paper was teeming with stories of dissolution and hardship. Over an 18-page
folio, I read about dispossessed schoolchildren in North

Carolina whose families had suffered mortgage defaults and foreclosures; Kenyans from Lake Turkana who had recently filled the slums of Nairobi after a prolonged summer drought; impoverished Bulgarian farmers who'd been victimized by governmental corruption and scandal; shopkeepers from Gabon attempting to rebuild their businesses after they'd been torched during election riots; a Mexican "Thriller" dance marathon organized to help allay tensions suffered during a record year of drug-related violence; the resignation of the Taiwanese prime minister after his inept handling of Typhoon Morakut left thousands of people displaced; the nomadic necessities of Sri Lanka's Tamil community; an incarcerated Californian lamenting how the world's economic crisis had led to the winnowing of food allotments in prison; four separate stories about the rootlessness of war-torn Afghanis; the largesse of rapper Ludacris, who donated 20 cars to contest winners chosen from over 4,000 laid-off workers; and the new novel by writer E.L. Doctorow, which documents the life of New York brothers who are notorious hoarders and who live in squalor until a newspaper tower collapses, killing one of them.

In the past, my encounters with the homeless and the dispossessed had been mostly limited to struggling artists and road-bound minstrels—people living on the fringes of art whom I'd met while travelling with my Canadian rock band. But my experiences weren't exclusive to life on the road. There was Irene, for instance, a former Cuban soap opera actress who'd fled her country after being threatened by the government for a controversial documentary she'd made.

Janet and I met her after answering the door one winter's evening. The first thing she asked us was whether or not she could have an old futon that we'd put at the curb. We told her that she could, and as we turned around to throw on our winter coats, she started crying. My wife consoled her while I stood there feeling awkward and bewildered. We helped her carry the bed over our heads and shoulders to her basement apartment like a lonely parade float. Afterwards, she returned to our home, and we talked for a while. She told us about her government's oppression, how they'd threatened her with a lifetime jail sentence, and how she'd sought asylum here after attending a conference in Ottawa. We made plans to get together, but, a few months later, without notice, Irene moved away.

Many years passed before I saw her again, sitting with her husband on the subway. It was the dreary heart of February, and they had the hoods of their parkas pulled tightly around their faces, shading their eyes. I moved to talk to them, but Irene could barely speak. At their feet lay two shopping bags filled with their belongings. I asked how things were going, and she said, "Not well. It is very hard. My husband is sad, having had to leave Cuba." Her eyes had turned hard and cold, drained of their soft Caribbean light. Her arms, which once butterflied when she spoke, sat motionless at her sides. When she reached her stop, I said goodbye, and then she and her husband disappeared into the muscle of the city.

Irene wasn't the only one. In my recreational hockey league there was a referee named Jim MacTavish. Jim was a good guy and a good ref. No one ever had anything bad to say against him. He ran games in a calm, friendly, and communicative way, as opposed to simply policing the ice. He was one of the few officials who showed up at the league's social events, and whenever it was time to make hockey cards for the league's players, there was always a square of cardboard reserved for Jim.

Then, one summer, Jim stopped showing up to his assigned games. League organizers were unable to locate him. Some time later, he was found living on his own in the parks and alleyways of Parkdale, Toronto's hardscrabble west-end corridor. One league official, who lived in the area, asked Jim if he needed a place to sleep, but Jim refused, his old demons having found their way back into his life. Knowing him as I did, I never would have suspected that his troubles ran so deep. He'd kept his problems secret, not wanting to burden his friends with them. Jim was the father of two children, both of them unaware of his condition. He'd been divorced and, before he disappeared, he'd broken up with his girlfriend. There was nobody left for him but himself.

One evening, news reached the league that a man resembling Jim had been found floating off Port Credit harbour, along the shoreline of Lake Ontario. The coroner reported that his body had been drifting in the water for weeks. At his memorial, a friend told us that whenever they talked about death, Jim told him that when it was his time to go, he wanted to swim into the lake and just vanish. To his friend, Jim had just been bullshitting—as we all do—about our mortality, stupid drunken babbling that you forget about the next morning. Looking back, those around him should have seen signs of his demise, but the homeless, the jobless, and those who are torn apart from their families often descend in silence, too proud to ask anything of others, too weak and fatigued to cry for help.

The greatest concentration of homeless men and women in Toronto can be found at the corner of one of Toronto's most

notorious intersections—Queen and Sherbourne—bordered
by the Good Shepherd Shelter, a row of suspicious-looking
coffee shops, a busy Aboriginal health centre, and, around
the corner, the darkened windows of the Artatorture tattoo
parlour. At the heart of this intersection also sits the John
Innes Community Recreation Centre, a city-run gymnasium
that gives way to a field—Moss Park—stretched out behind
it. Outside the centre, a handful of men and women crumples
across dead grass lawns while another handful scours the
sidewalks looking for cigarette butts as if searching for lost
teeth. Across the street, the mentally damaged walk up the
steps of the shelter, pull on its locked doors, shuffle down
the steps towards the road, then shuffle back up the steps
moments later. Lots of nothing occurs at a constant and fre-
netic pace, whether it's the crowded patrons of a blue-smoke
donut shop not eating; people sitting on a curb outside the
adjacent Moss Park hockey rink not playing; or men standing around an employment centre not working. All of this is
played out under the gaze of new condominiums rising to the
southwest and staring unblinking over the corridor's shelters,
recovery centres, and dive bars.

I'd passed the centre many times before—years ago, I'd
even lived in a building a few blocks south, far enough away
to feel as if what was happening around John Innes was happening in another city—but I always kept walking. Then,
one day, while crossing Moss Park heading north, I noticed
a clutch of homeless men and women—eyes downcast, faces
weathered—hanging out behind the centre wearing duct-
taped runners and wrong-sized Value Village sweats. At the
centre of their group, a man was crouching and holding a
soccer ball. Suddenly, he flung the ball to the grass, and those

who'd once appeared infirm, addled, stoned, sad, damaged, and broken sprang to life, following the ball's flight as if it were a great bird cruising above them. To watch them play, you never would have known that Krystal Bell, an 18-year-old runaway from Regent Park, had left her adopted family in Kitchener to live aimlessly in sheds and garages, on friends' couches, and in shitty apartments run by creeps with a thing for sad girls; or that Billy Pagonis had been a former soccer pro before losing his family, friends, and business to a pain-killer and cocaine addiction. There, on the wet sod of the early May lawn, the players' transformation seemed wild and real, and my longstanding belief in the magic of play and the redemptive properties of sport were confirmed. And it was happening in my city.

I returned to the field a few more times, and, eventually, I got to know Krystal and Billy and the others. Their games were part of the centre's homeless soccer program—also known as Street Soccer Canada—which was run by three men—Rob Uddenberg, Paul Gregory, and Cristian Burcea—on a largely after-hours and volunteer basis. Paul told me that the players were preparing for a national homeless championship tournament in Calgary a few months later, and he seemed to appreciate my interest, considering the singularity of their approach and the difficulties inherent in running a program that was stigmatized because of the nature of its participants.

After I had been hanging around long enough, Paul—a bespectacled, middle-aged social-housing advocate with a soft voice and steady demeanour that motored at, but never exceeded, the speed limit—invited me to travel west to watch the players and write about them. He also said that the Homeless World Cup tournament was happening later that fall in Melbourne, Australia, and that Canada would be among 56 competing nations. I must have looked both delighted and astonished, having never heard of the tournament before. I told him that it sounded like the very thing that a sporting world bloated by excess and self-aggrandizement might have needed and the perfect way to frame a community of suffering to those of us for whom sports was also a social and spiritual balm.

"The circumstances of the world become a lot clearer once you meet the athletes and watch them play," he said. "There are homeless players who've gone on to play professionally, and professional athletes—like Billy—who've become homeless and are playing for the first time in years. You should really see this sort of thing for yourself." I told him that it sounded like an incredible event. Then he asked if I'd want to come to Melbourne, too.

1

WHAT

TEAMS DO

I ACCEPTED PAUL'S INVITATION and flew to Calgary for the national summer tournament. There, I walked into an argument between three homeless men stalking each other on the steps of the grey building that housed the event's gymnasium and indoor soccer fields. First, Devon—a nearly toothless Jamaican Canadian who suffered from mental health and addiction issues—called Billy, the recovering OxyContin addict, a douchebag. Then Eric—the team's goaltender, who moved about like a willow sagging after a long rain—called Devon a cocksucker. Then Devon chased Eric around the parking lot, hucking an orange at him and growling "Man, don't call another man cocksucker." Devon skulked behind the rear of the building, looking out occasionally to see if the goalie was coming back for more. But Eric had returned to his pre-championship pickup game, which is where the argument had started: Devon wanting to play, being rebuffed by Billy, swearing at Billy, then being sworn at before Eric called him a cocksucker, at which point Devon grabbed the orange, then a can of Coke, which slung inside Devon's trouser pocket.

The Calgary tournament had been staged to give Paul, the manager, and Cristian, the coach, a chance to survey all of the homeless players in one fell swoop. While neither Devon nor Eric were eligible to play—they'd already competed for Canada in previous world tournaments; Homeless World Cup (HWC) rules stipulate that players can only represent their country once—the coaches were considering naming Billy to the national team, as well as Krystal, who'd recently moved in with her brother, Jason, in Toronto. After the argument played itself out, I went inside the gym, where I found Krystal sitting on a set of metal bleachers, eating a granola bar and staring at the court.

"I was adopted when I was two," she told me from the stands. "My mom dropped me off at my brother's friend's house—his name was Soldier—and that was when Children's Aid got involved and helped me find a home. I don't know who my dad was, but I kept in contact with my mom and grandparents. Sometimes my adopted parents would drive me back to Regent Park to see my mom, and I remember being so excited going through the hallways of the building waiting to see her. My only two memories of her are the day I found out she'd died, and visiting her one time when she was standing in the doorway of the building telling me that she loved me. I didn't really know what her life was about until years later. When I was 16, my grandmother gave me a box of letters that our social worker had written to my family, describing how my mother was a prostitute, how she was addicted to drugs, and that she'd died of AIDS as a result of being a sex worker in Regent Park. She'd been born in Trinidad and came to Canada, but because my grandfather lived in the States, she went back and forth from country to country. Things were bad where my grandpa was living, and she got drawn in, overwhelmed and tempted by things in the big city. There were rules at my grandma's house, but not so much in the States. Sometimes I think that if I were a little bit older— that if I wasn't just a baby when the problems started to happen—I might have been able to help her, to make a difference. If I could go back in time and change it, I would. But the way I look at it, everything happens for a reason. Maybe I'm able to do all of the things because she never got to. She's in my heart. She'll never leave me."

We sat in silence for a moment as a few players began drifting onto the court. Then Krystal clasped her hands together and said, "I really hope the coaches choose me for the team. I mean, Australia. It would be my dream to go to Australia." She paused and then she said: "Actually, it would be my dream to go anywhere in the world. But Australia. Man..."

At the end of the three-day event, Krystal made it easy for the coaches to select her. Before the tournament's final game—which Toronto lost to Vancouver in a thrilling shootout (there were also teams from Calgary and a three-person representation from the Old Brewery mission in Montreal)— the players were asked to talk about their experiences in Calgary. Cristian—who, because he was young and track-suited, talked shit with the players, if in a tone measured with a smile—told them that if they had anything to say, now was the time.

At first, they were quiet, but you could tell what they were thinking. By this point in the event, Eric, the goaltender—a tempestuous, six-foot-two crack addict whose gaunt face was drawn with the perpetual charcoal of a person too defeated to groom himself—had begun to wear on his teammates, and they'd frozen him out after the final game. During the meeting, he was the first to speak, telling his teammates in a low voice how disappointed he was that they hadn't congratulated him after many of the games. "Every other team does it," he said. "The first thing they do is congratulate the goalie, but all you guys do is walk away."

The players rolled their eyes. They may have been exasperated with Eric's popgun temper, but the real issue was about more than just Eric. Their lives were so difficult and complicated that together those lives produced an entanglement of fear, self-doubt, sadness, neurosis, and anger, a powder keg of suffering that was defused only when the players were working together on the court. Once the games had ended, their endorphins flattened and their bodies—which had tasted a natural, physical high for the first time in ages—sought to continue the tourney's competitive stimulation. The result was anger and revolt and confrontation. And really, because it had already been a huge struggle—and a great triumph—for these players to simply make their flight to Calgary, they lacked the emotional reserve to deal with the massive issues in each other's lives. So when Eric bared his heart, there was little energy or impetus left to console him.

After Eric finished talking, the coach moved to send the team back to their hotel. But Krystal turned to her teammates and said, "Eric's right, guys. No matter what happens in the game, we should go up and thank our goalie. We may not like what we have to put up with—and not just with Eric; we can all get on each other's nerves—but we're a team, and we should be able to count on each other all the time."

Nobody else had anything else to say.

"I mean, it's what teams do," she added.

"So, you know, let's start doing it."

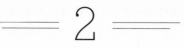

COLD
TURKEY
SOCCER

For the organizers, putting together Homeless Team Canada was never easy, not with a modest budget (all of Team Canada's funding comes from private donations) and the responsibility of obtaining the necessary documents from homeless men and women. When Paul first discovered that the tournament would require travel to Australia, he remembered past times, when even a seven-hour journey had proven nearly impossible for some players. There was a fellow from Toronto named Angelo Variano, who was nearly penniless, living on dumpster scraps and shelter broth. But because the fall tournament came on the heels of one of the street person's annual bounties—Toronto's million-strong Gay Pride Parade—Angelo paid for his ninety-dollar passport to the 2007 Copenhagen event after gathering bottles strewn about the city. Emboldened by his efforts, he decided to use the team's transcontinental flight to Denmark to quit methadone, cold turkey. For the eight-hour flight, he sat bathed in a terrible sweat, coiling, then uncoiling, next to his manager, from whom he'd kept his airborne rehab a secret.

There was another player, Max, who, on the journey to the Homeless World Cup in 2006 in Cape Town, locked himself in the airplane's bathroom, driven to isolation by the voices he was hearing in his head. Max lived on a floodplain in the Don Valley in Toronto, a great mohawk of trees that cleaves the city's north-south parkway. He subsisted on whatever food he could scrounge, and every now and then, when his food supply grew scarce, he was forced to come into the city. Paul found him greasy and bearded on the streets, so he invited him to John Innes, where he mentioned the homeless-team program. Paul was certain he'd be rebuffed, but Max accepted the invitation and was eventually chosen to play for Team Canada. Although he never spoke about his mental condition, Paul said, "I knew there were issues there, I just didn't know how severe." Paul sat outside the bathroom door along with the flight attendants and murmured to Max, helping him get through the ordeal. Max competed in the tournament and competed well. After he got back to Toronto, he thanked Paul, headed back to his tarpaulin home on the floodplain, and was never heard from again.

Another of the national team's organizational complications came from having to work with regional managers who were responsible for clearing players from their respective programs. Paul and Cristian had chosen two Vancouverites for the team—a Mexican immigrant named Manny and a Aboriginal Canadian named John—but much to their chagrin, the West Coast homeless chapter proved to be wanting in the manner in which they processed—or didn't process— their documents. Despite a barrage of emails from Toronto requesting information about how things were proceeding, they instead found their inbox filled with press announce- ments and invitations to upcoming fundraisers. Cristian had warned Vancouver of the Aussies' and the Homeless World Cup's organizational vigilance, but they responded with tum- bleweeds. The Team Canada managers grew livid at Vancou- ver's unresponsiveness, not only because losing their invitees would burn their budget and gut their roster, but because it would mean a return to the bedbugs for two of their hopeful charges. If there had been excess cash, which there never was, Paul might have been able to rally the correct documents for new players at such a late stage, but Australian immigration laws—and resulting HWC protocol—required almost double the paperwork of past tourneys, 60 pages per player. Cristian received a terse email from organizers claiming that Team Canada's inclusion in the event was in jeopardy. Things were eventually resolved, but the coaches lay awake at night won- dering whether almost $15,000 worth of plane tickets—a large portion of the team's budget—would go to waste, to say nothing of denying Manny and John the opportunity to join them on their journey to the bottom of the world.

At one point, Paul and Cristian had considered bringing another Vancouver player to Melbourne, a small, grey-haired, fiftysomething Arab man named Sam who wore 1970s high- school gym shorts and carried around a shopping bag filled with shoes, socks, jerseys, and three sets of daily newspapers. But Sam's papers were incomplete, the result of having lived like so many other refugees, a man without a country to call his own.

I'd met Sam on my first day in Calgary, and after I asked him about his life, he took me by the elbow and paraded me to a set of empty bleachers, where he unfurled the story of his life. Sam was born in Palestine, where his parents once owned a large tract of land—eight million dollars' worth, he said—on the disputed West Bank. But they'd been forced to scatter as a result of the war in the Middle East. Because his family was able to retain at least a portion of its wealth, his parents sent him to school in California, where he studied world literature. He finished school with a degree and a book idea, which eventually became *American Triumph*, the story of a young American woman who helps Afghani rebels turn back the Soviet war machine. People liked the book; it sold a few thousand copies. For the next year, Sam toured America, talking about his work, his life, and the legacy of his family.

Then came 9/11. One afternoon in California, Sam was sitting at a Denny's eating breakfast with three newspapers spread open at his table. Two men approached his booth: thugs wearing sunglasses, cologne, and silk socks. Can we have a word? *I wrote 80,000 words. Pick one.* Hands to shoulder, they walked him across the restaurant into the daylight, where he was bagged and thrown into the ass-end of an unmarked van. Thugs. Thugs with a pension. They threw him into the piss and murder of the Laredo County jail, where the author of *American Triumph* languished for eight months.

Sam wrote. He wrote to judges, attorneys, counsellors, journalists. Then, one day, the guards delivered him a note, unchaining the cell door as they passed it to him. An immigration judge had granted his release. While being processed, the plaid shirt that he'd worn to his arraignment hung loose at the shoulder, his pants barely hooked to his hip. A policeman in plain clothes stood at his desk, quilted his fingers at his waist, then looked Sam in the eye before looking away at the photograph of America's commander-in-chief hanging beyond the writer's shoulder. Then he told him that he was sorry.

Sam got the fuck out of the USA. Like Ray Charles, he rode a bus to Seattle, then crossed the border through the forest. He came into Canada and found work as a paperless labourer living in a shelter. If he carried around a scythe of bitterness, you couldn't see it. Before leaving Calgary, he approached me and said: "I've written two more manuscripts. I'm proud of both. One is about Ireland. Will you help get it published?" He gave me his novel, but Sam never made it to Melbourne, nor did any of the other Vancouver players. Days before the team was scheduled to depart for Australia, Paul finally reached the managers of the West Coast program. They told him that they planned on marching with the men down to the BC parliament, where they would demand they provide papers to help them get to Oz. Of course, they came up empty. In a tournament where Canada would play against teams with eight to ten players on their roster (the game required four men a side, competing on a 16x22 metre court for two seven-minute halves), Paul and Cristian would be bringing only Billy and Krystal, plus two other players from Calgary. In the end, they decided that it was better to travel somewhere with half of a team than go nowhere at all.

3

JOURNEY

TO OZ

THE SKY WAS grey and wet with rain as the players gathered at John Innes on the morning of their trip to Oz. I found Billy sitting outside on the steps of the centre, a hood pulled over his head to protect himself from the wind and the rain. Billy was the only former professional player on the team, as well as the best and most experienced athlete. He also had the distinction of playing on both Team Canada and Homeless Team Canada, and when I pointed this out, he said, irreverently, "Hey, I just love to play the game. What happens outside of it is secondary." He was the same age as me—45—and Greek ("*way* Greek," said Krystal), sometimes even using his given name, Basile, instead of its Anglicized cousin. If the faces of the men around the centre bore the crust of defeat, Billy possessed at least the verisimilitude of a person who'd competed at an athletically high level. The first time I'd met him, his face was glistening with sweat, having just run laps on the centre's track. It was the first time in years he'd been close to his playing weight, his bullish shoulders and broad chest returning after a long descent into addiction. Only his face—which still carried the excess weight of his sedentary years—belied the fact that he'd once possessed a formidable athletic physique.

After years of playing pro soccer—both domestically, with the North York Rockets, and internationally, with Team Canada as well as club teams in Switzerland and Austria—Billy had retired so that he could take over the ownership of Uncle Harry's Fish and Chips, a restaurant that his father had started after emigrating from Greece. "The restaurant was my parents' place before I started running it," he said. "They wanted to retire, and I figured that it would be a good thing to do after my playing career ended. In 2006, I put over $100,000 into it, and it was a huge success. Man, I was living large. The casinos were sending limousines for me; I was throwing down huge bets, huge money. Then, in 2008, I transferred the place over to my father for a dollar because I was a mess. My parents had to come home from their retirement place in Greece to take it back. I was making $8,000 profit a week, but I was killing myself, pulling 100 hours a week and taking painkillers—OxyContins—which users call 'hillbilly heroin.' It all started while sitting around one night in a bar. I was complaining to my friends about my headaches, so someone said, 'Here, try these.' They worked; it was like a miracle. Pretty soon, there wasn't a day when I wasn't on them, and because I felt good, I got into other stuff, mostly cocaine, which I'd done before, but never in such quantities. After a while, I saw what this was doing to me, so I tried to quit. I had joint pain, and I was vomiting. When I was off the stuff, I couldn't walk more than three feet without feeling as if my life was about to end. So I went back to it. I went back hard and I stayed there.

"Eventually, I lost contact with my friends and I stopped talking to my parents. Instead of getting help, I tried quitting again. I self-medicated by smoking weed, lots of it. I smoked weed and never left the apartment. I ate constantly for a month. I ate like a pig and slept and smoked and I gained a ton of weight. I comatosed myself. It worked, but I couldn't do anything else. I was like a corpse. I was breathing, eating, and I was alive. But that's all I was. One night, I got into a fight with my girlfriend, and they threw me in jail. That was my wake up call. I went to CAMH [Centre for Addiction and Mental Health] and they helped me get clean. It was a horrible experience, but that's it. I'm done with that shit. I'm going to Australia. And let me tell you," he said, stabbing the air, "I'm going to fill the net."

Despite his efforts to maintain a kind of normalcy, Billy's life was still in flux. A court order forced him to live with his former girlfriend, the person who'd charged him with domestic assault after he destroyed their apartment. It was a vengeful relationship. She toyed mercilessly with Billy's recovery, smoking pot and hosting drunken parties in an attempt to tease him back into his old habits. "These days, I get up and leave there as early as I can and I come home as late as I can. The less time I spend around her the better, but if I don't go home, all she has to do is pick up the phone and call the police, and then I'm back in jail. I'm at her mercy. I'm fucked." A few weeks before leaving for Melbourne, Billy's patience thinned and he hit the streets, spending a handful of winter evenings on his own. "I just walked around the city," he said, "then slept at the counter of my friend's donut shop. I got back to the house just in time to convince her not to report me. But I was this close," he said, making a wafer with his fingers. "This close."

Paul and Cristian privately worried that Billy lacked the discipline needed to play in the HWC. One of the conditions of Billy's parole was that he enrol in anger management counselling—he was only now just finishing the program—and the coaches were concerned that putting him in a competitive environment against foreign teams might open old wounds. Because I was the only one who'd seen the fight between Billy, Devon, and Eric, Cristian asked me for details. I told him that, after the dust had settled, Billy walked by himself to the edge of the centre's lot, where he lay under a tree to cool down. To the naked eye, it might not have looked like much, but for Billy, it showed a certain resolve and commitment to change his life as best he could.

Neither Billy nor Krystal had any idea what the next ten days would bring. They were going to Australia—the land of sunshine, beaches, cans of Fosters, *Crocodile Dundee*, and kangaroos—but, more than that, the world was going there, too: 600 homeless athletes competing over seven days. Canada had never won the tournament, but Cristian and Paul said that winning wasn't important; it was the revitalization of the players' lives by which the team's success was measured. They could point to several examples, and, in one instance, they could even produce a player on-hand: Bradley Tough, who worked across the street from John Innes as a therapist and counsellor at the Aboriginal social centre.

Before joining the program, Brad moved aimlessly across the country—sleeping on his sister's couch, meeting people he shouldn't have met, doing things he shouldn't have done—until he found the homeless team playing one afternoon in Moss Park. Brad accompanied Team Canada to Edinburgh, Scotland, where he smudged his face with war paint and competed as the tournament's first Aboriginal player. "I told him back then," said Cris, "that he had the opportunity to destroy all of those Native stereotypes, and that he could be a role model for a community that sometimes finds it hard to integrate into programs like ours."

While Brad was competing abroad, his grandfather fell ill in Saskatchewan, but from his deathbed, he saw a CBC feature on his grandson's trip to Scotland. The grandfather roused himself long enough to demand that the nurses find coverage of the HWC on television. Of course, they couldn't, and the grandfather passed away while Brad was overseas. When he returned, Brad went back to Saskatchewan, reconciled with his family, and visited his grandfather's gravesite, where he slung his tournament medal over the old man's tombstone.

Before hauling their bags into one of the rec centre employees' cars bound for the airport, Billy, Krystal, Paul, and Cris said goodbye to Eric, who'd come to see the team off to Melbourne (they'd be joined later on the journey by the two other players from Calgary). Eric's crack addiction had lasted the better part of two decades, but he'd recently secured an assisted-living apartment with five other men who, when I visited him, moved about the house with a heavy, if unseen, presence. Although he was tall and great limbed, Eric moved around awkwardly, as if his bones somehow didn't quite fit. Still, whenever I watched him compete on the court during the centre's twice-weekly games, the ravages of his addiction faded away as he bent on one knee to stop shots, or stretched across the crease to knock down a ball with his gloved hands. In Cape Town in 2006, he was named the tournament's Best Goalkeeper. He'd stopped 17 consecutive penalty kicks and had returned to Canada festooned with ribbons, medals, and a trophy.

Wearing an old pair of track pants and a blackened windbreaker, Eric walked up to Krystal, who was sitting in the centre's lounge, and handed her a small plastic packet.

"Take it," he said. "You might need this. It's a gift."

Krystal smiled and told him, "No, Eric, I can't. I'm getting on a plane."

"Go ahead, take it. It's really no problem."

"No, Eric, really."

She handed the package back to Eric. It disappeared in the pocket of his windbreaker. Later, at the airport, someone asked Krystal if she knew what Eric had given her. She said she didn't; she hadn't looked at it.

"I know what was in the package," pffffted Billy. "Drugs. What else would be in a package from Eric?"

After Krystal had refused the package, Eric turned and looked at the others gathered in the room.

"Well, at least take my gloves," he said.

Cristian told him: "Eric, we're bringing so many things on the trip we don't have room for your gloves."

Eric looked crestfallen.

"You've got all of this other stuff, why not the gloves?" he asked.

"They'll have gloves there. Besides, we don't even know who our goaltender is. We'll probably use an Australian," said Cris.

"Which is why you should bring me."

"You know we can't bring you."

"I know. It's a stupid bullshit rule."

"But it's the rule," said Cristian.

One of the centre's outreach employees came into the room and produced a large paper shopping bag stuffed with enormous tubes of sunscreen.

"My gift to Krystal was better than that," said Eric.

Holding one of the tubes, Cristian told the employee: "You guys never spare on the expense, do you?"

Everyone in the room laughed; everyone except Eric. You could tell that it hurt him to see his friends joking and messing around before their journey. He looked across the room at me and held out his gloves. I zippered open a pouch on the exterior of my suitcase and pushed them in.

"Hey, Eric, thanks again, okay?" said Krystal.

"Just go get 'em out there. Don't take any shit from anyone just because you're a woman," he said.

"Don't worry, Eric. Whatever they throw at me, it's nothing I haven't seen before."

"Okay. And remember: *"Boombaye! Boombaya!"* he said, shouting his favourite goal crease cheer.

"'Boombaye, boombaya,' got it, Eric," said Krystal, showing him her fist before closing her suitcase.

The players said goodbye to Eric and filed into their respective cars. I drove to the airport with Krystal, her brother, Jason, and Jason's girlfriend. For the trip, Krystal climbed into the space between the front seats and wrapped her arms around what was left of her birth family, nuzzling her face against her brother's neck as if committing his scent to memory. Because Krystal had been homeless during much of her recent life, she seemed both young and old, naive yet wise, her eyes filled with equal measures of wonder and suspicion. While she possessed the vulnerability of a teenager, her body moved with an air of defiance, as if, at any moment, another force might try and overtake her. She spoke carefully but authoritatively, her voice belling the way the carriage on a typewriter does after reaching its length. While everyone else filled their time at the airport saying stupid soccer-team-on-the-road shit to each other, Krystal drew herself into a teenage cocoon surrounded by the necessary accoutrements: trashy magazines, chocolate bars, a bouquet of pens tied together with coloured elastics, fluffy slippers and flip-flops, a sheaf of homework (Krystal had gone back to high school to complete her grade 12 degree), an iPod loaded with songs by Nas, and some bottled water. Her neck was marked with a pair of tattoos—one, a set of initials commemorating her mother, who'd died when Krystal was two; and the other, a flower for her grandmother. Occasionally, she'd look around the airport and say things like *I can't believe this!* and *This is amazing!* while holding a spiral notepad with photos pasted on the cover in which she wrote down her thoughts in looping schoolgirl script—WILL YOU SHINE WHEN THE SPOTLIGHT HITS YOU?—sometimes in verse, sometimes not. One colour photograph showed her two nephews—Jason's kids—as well as a photo of Krystal at age four, crouching with her elbows leaning on a soccer ball. "I played for the Nitros," she told me before flipping the notepad closed. Another photograph, which she carried in her back pocket, was creased and yellowed. It showed Krystal as a baby being cradled in the lap of a beautiful young woman in a red summer dress.

Her mom.

WHEN WE REACHED the airport, Paul told the players what to tell customs and US immigration—that they were travelling to Australia for a soccer tournament—reminding them never to use the word "homeless" unless they had to. Because Billy had a criminal record and was travelling on a special Visa, there were fears that authorities would interrogate the team, as had happened in the past. In some cases, homeless teams had been detained for days at the airport, but after questions about the players' special dispensation, they passed through immigration and we soon found ourselves waiting at the gate to board the plane.

At the airport, Billy never stopped talking. He commented on life the way a track announcer calls a race, including every movement and building to a crescendo of full caps and exclamation points. He was all Mediterranean flurry and braggadocio, built like an oak wardrobe with a broad chest. He could take any subject and weave it into an anecdote, slapping your arm or poking the side of your chair when he couldn't reach a body part, making sure your thoughts hadn't drifted. He had the ego of a former star player, and few moments passed in which he didn't ensure that he was the focus of the group's attention. But he leavened his bluster with moments of self-deprecation and honesty. His life was an open book— a tragicomedy—whose pages were forever fluttering in the breeze.

Walking to the departure gate, Billy paused between stories, looked around, held up a finger, and spoke a single word: "Methadone."

I wasn't sure whether discussing methadone was part of the same federal regulations that forbid the mention of bomb and guns, but, just in case, I whispered to him that it might not be the wisest thing to talk about narcotics before hopping on a transcontinental flight.

He looked at me indignantly. "Methadone," he repeated.

"You see, when the junkies went for methadone in jail, they wouldn't swallow it. Well, they'd swallow some of it, but then they'd spit the rest into their friend's mouth, and take his twenty bucks. When the doctors and guards found out, the junkies started regurgitating it, and then they sold *that*. Now, when you get methadone in jail, they make you wait twenty minutes in a room so you process it. They got wise, see, and now the junkies can't do it anymore."

"When were you ever in prison with junkies?" asked Paul.

"Mistaken identity, a federal house," he said, taking a long breath.

"But I thought you only did time for domestic violence."

"This was before."

"Before?" said Paul.

"Relax. I got sprung. I did four days. Four. It was horrible. Scary. It was 1989, credit card fraud, a guy who had the same name as me with family members who had the same name as my family, only he had a sister, Jennifer, I think, which I didn't have, so I got off. But my lawyer was in Jamaica, so he couldn't get me released and it was a long weekend. I was in a three by three cell, no contact for 23 hours. My parents were begging for me to get out, but they couldn't do nothing. There were murderers in there, one guy, Rico, long hair and beard. His wife was missing for two years and they couldn't find the body. He cut her up and put her body parts in glass jars, to keep them fresh, I guess. I don't know. He hid them in the walls. Then he sold the house, but the new owners decided to renovate. They found her, and he got convicted.

He was in there. They were all in there. My roommate was a guy called Fat Jack, who ran the cantina. He protected me because I had 1,500 bucks in my prison account and I paid him off. Inmates communicated by tapping on the pipes, tapping in code. They do this thing they called fishing, tying notes to twine that they remove from their pillowcases and sheets. One guy would send out a message and another guy would retrieve it with a toothbrush tied to a piece of twine sent across the prison floor. During a meal, a guy asked me if I wanted any candy, but I got up and moved to the other end of the hall. If you take their candy, it means you're their bitch. Fat Jack told me this. Fat Jack was all right, but thank God I got the fuck out."

On the plane, I sat behind Billy and listened to him talk for most of the 16-hour flight. It wasn't until we were halfway across the Pacific Ocean that he fell silent, strapping on his headphones to watch *Mamma Mia!*. I had wondered what it might take to silence him: maybe an earthquake or nuclear strike? Perhaps a global technological meltdown? But a musical comedy starring Meryl Streep I hadn't considered.

Krystal spent most of her time scribbling in her notepad. Occasionally, she held up a page for me to see:

GRANDMA YOU ARE THE ONE AND I AM GOING FOR YOU

or

AUSTRALIA DUNNO WHAT ABOUT TO HIT THEM

4

WALTER MITTY AND A DILDO

DURING THE TEAM'S connection in Los Angeles, the team was joined by the Calgarian homeless players: Jerry Stenhouse, an aging seat-cushion salesman who'd become homeless while chasing an elusive dream; and a 24-year-old Moroccan immigrant who asked me to call him Juventus. When I told him that I would be writing a book about the team's trip, he told me, in a low, North African murmur, "You cannot use my real name. There are some things that neither you, nor anyone else, can know." Both players were exhausted, having had to travel from Calgary to Los Angeles before heading to Melbourne. I tried engaging Juventus in conversation, but this proved difficult. He'd spent the last few years wandering around Canada looking for a home and employment. His last job had been as a carpenter, but the sharp decline in Calgary's building boom had forced him out on the streets.

Juventus was a light-skinned Arab. He had a thin moustache and crop of black hair that sat teased high on his head in the style of a young Cab Calloway. He possessed the soft, careful ways of his people, and he often prefaced his thoughts by holding up a single finger to speak, then saying, "You know…" before imparting a kind of measured desert wisdom mirrored in the book that he carried with him, Paolo Coelho's *The Alchemist*. On the field, he was a quick-footed player who'd impressed management with his velvet skills and unflappable, professional comportment. Discussions about his life always ended abruptly, leaving one with the feeling of having read a second-hand novel with important chapters torn out. One of Calgary's homeless coaches told Paul that Juventus was a good teammate but that he sometimes disappeared for long periods of time.

After arriving in Oz, the team was absorbed into a cloud of track suits: Romanian, Dutch, Greek, and Kenyan players arriving for the tournament. The Americans landed soon after and were seen collecting their bags. Paul and Cristian had allowed themselves one competitive maxim. "We can't lose to the USA," they said, gritting their teeth. As the other athletes paraded past, Billy grumbled, "These guys, wearing their track suits and everything. Our team, we don't even have a goalie. We're like, all ragtag or somethin'."

"You're not 'like all ragtag or somethin','" I told him. "You are ragtag."

"There's a difference?" he asked.

"A big one," I said.

"Yeah. Well, I just wish we had a goalie."

Team Canada boarded a bus, and before long, they'd settled at their temporary hotel in St. Kilda, about 30 minutes from the city centre (they would move into Melbourne

University once the tournament officially started, two days later). St. Kilda is a beachside stretch of bookstores, bars, and cake shops. Along one of its sandy curves sits the Luna Park fairgrounds, with its laughing clown-face entrance and the world's oldest roller coaster, built on wooden struts and painted Coney Island white. St. Kilda also contained Melbourne's greatest preponderance of sex shops. One evening, I strolled past Jerry's room and heard a voice saying "You're looking super hot tonight!" and "Hey, nice rack, baby!" Walking into the room, I saw that he had purchased a novelty doorbell from one of the sex shops.

"Here, check it out!" he said, forcing the noisemaker at me.

"Honey, you look good enough to eat!"

"Geez, no one's ever been that nice to me," I told it.

"I know, I know," he said. "Aren't they great?"

Jerry was an unassuming nebbish who'd suffered financial dissolution after the failure of several business ventures. He was a 21st-century homeless figure: mentally sound, with no addiction issues, but he'd been thrown to the mat after making the wrong choices in a capitalist society that encourages risk.

Jerry looked like a ripe tomato with stems for legs. It was no accident that he visited St. Kilda's sex shops more than any other player. He told me that he wanted to make sure that his latest brainstorm didn't already exist: vibrators and dildos with soccer ball and basketball penis heads. "People will love them. Don't you think they'd they love them?" he asked. But I resisted answering, not wanting to establish myself as someone who was either pro- or anti-novelty penis heads. I told him that I thought he might really be on to something and left it at that.

If Juventus had been loath to discuss the past, Jerry made it seem as if he had no past at all. When I asked him questions about his life—where he was born, if he'd been married, what his upbringing was like—he said, "Maybe after the tournament. Maybe we'll sit down and talk then, okay?" It was surprising to hear this after spending time with Billy and Krystal, who had spoken candidly about their lives. But whether or not Jerry was attempting to hide the events of his past seemed less important once I saw how determinedly he forced himself beyond them, parading blithely through life as if in a rainstorm with only a bent umbrella to sustain his balance. There was a little bit of Walter Mitty in Jerry; he was able to cast off the wreckage of his past so that he might continue moving forward. He refused to acknowledge the hands of fate for fear of being slowed by them.

Still, his life was as mysterious as Juve's, and even though I suspected that I might never know the truth, the search for it proved no less interesting. Before coming to Melbourne, Paul told me that Jerry's recent obsession had been a new kind of seat cushion made from space-age fibres. In between episodes of couch-surfing, he'd spent time hawking the invention to local manufacturers, but the process had nearly ruined him. After hiring a team of lawyers to arrange the paperwork required to give him full control over his product, the lawyers had secretly acquired the cushion's patent. When I asked Jerry if he was trying to win back his patent while undomiciled, his soft, pouchlike face and long, hopeful eyes hardened for a moment. "Undomiciled?" he said, brusquely. "No, that's wrong. I've always had a home. Always."

When I told this to Paul, he said, "I'm not sure what he means. I know that he lived at Keith's [the Calgary homeless team's manager's] house and that Keith got him a job because he didn't have one. At least that's what Keith says."

"But Jerry says that he never lived at Keith's," I said.

"With a lot of guys, the lines blur between fact and fiction," he replied, sighing. "When they find themselves in difficult situations, they're often too ashamed or afraid to admit what's happened to them, so they invent things. And sometimes, when they tell you their story, they leave a lot of things out. Big chunks of their lives go untold, and most people never really know the truth."

"But if Jerry was never really homeless, how did he end up playing for this team?"

"That's a good question," said Paul, wearily rubbing his face. "Maybe you can find out the real answer."

"But don't you have to be homeless to play in this tournament?"

"Yes, you do. Clearly," he said. "But you might have noticed, Dave. We only have four players."

LIKE MOST TEAMS before a tournament, the Canadians were drunk with hope and possibility. And sometimes they were just drunk. On their first night in Melbourne, they dined at a local fish and chip shop. Billy found out that the proprietor was from Athens, so he spent most of the meal laughing with him and swearing at him in Greek. After dinner, Krystal excused herself and threw up, too nervous to keep anything down. Later in the evening, on the hotel balcony, Billy popped open a beer, drew in a gasp of ocean air, spread his arms, and announced: "I'm gonna fill the net. My ankle feels good. I'm ready; we're all ready. For the first time since I was 35, I feel like I'm at the top of my game."

Cristian, who was the first to start drinking, got in on the act, too, swilling a succession of Blondes and pointing at three people at once while saying, "All of you guys have played in front of lots of people at a high level. You won't get shaken by the size of the event; no way, not you." I asked Paul whether he thought it was appropriate for the players—and management, for that matter—to drink alcohol, considering their issues with substance abuse, but he reminded me, "We're a soccer team who've come to play in a soccer tournament. We want to keep things as normal as possible. Beer and sports—at least in Canada—is normal. And by the way, would you like one?" He passed me an ale. I opened the bottle and leaned over the balcony railing, peering into St. Kilda's macramé of English gardens, courtyard homes, and wrought-iron lampposts, which, farther down, gave way to a seaside promenade and the great sweeping eye of the ocean.

I trusted that Paul knew what he was doing, although his approach, it turned out, was atypical among other homeless soccer managers. One of the first things the Finns had done after arriving in Melbourne was get themselves to an AA meeting, which they did once, sometimes twice a day. The Scots had enforced a team curfew, but, on their first night in Melbourne, three players had stayed out past midnight and were subsequently dropped from their opening match. The English were also forced to cancel a pre-tournament practice because of disciplinary measures, and already a Kenyan had gone missing from his team. In another year, one team had arrived with three recovering methadone addicts, whose addiction they babied by pouring them mugs of warm beer with breakfast each morning.

The first night in Oz, an American player named Tad—a former crystal meth addict from Texas—was discovered by teammates passed out in the washroom of a downtown bar. Even though the Americans were travelling with an entourage of 16 people—one counsellor for every other player—USA organizer Lawrence Cann wasn't fazed by the transgression. They would hold a faith-based meeting the following morning, he said, to address the issue. Paul, however, was unconvinced. "The guy's a surviving crystal meth addict. A few prayers is really gonna stop him from having a beer," he said.

Talk among the Canadians turned to strategy—how the team would use their substitutes in net and keep the forwards together—and everyone agreed that this was a plan to rival the genius of Guus Hiddink. The evening's revelry yielded two conclusions: not only would Team Canada almost certainly bring home a trophy, they'd also likely set the record for most beer consumed at a homeless sporting event.

At the end of their crystal ball session, Krystal told the team that the following day would mark the anniversary of her mom's death. Everyone grew quiet. You could see in Krystal's face her realization that, instead of marking this event alone in some lost corner of the city, or with friends she knew she would not keep, or while sleeping under a blanket in a bus shelter wondering what she'd done to deserve such a fate, she was paying tribute to her late mother with her friends, her teammates, while staring at the South Pacific ocean.

After a pause, she took a pull on her beer, then pushed it into the air, shouting, "CANADA IS IN AUSTRALIA!" her voicing carrying throughout the neighbourhood. Below her, an old woman in drooping knee socks who was shuffling along with her dog looked up, frowned gravely, and tsked the young Canadian.

"Sorry..." said Krystal, smiling and hiding her beer.

5

THE
SONG OF
INDIA

MEL YOUNG AND Harald Schmied—a Scotsman and an Austrian—dreamed up the
Homeless World Cup while attending a conference in 2002
that dealt with the future of street newspapers. There, they
hatched the idea of raising awareness about homelessness
through soccer. Although it was originally intended as a two-
nation challenge match, 18 countries ended up participating
in the first tournament in 2003 in Graz, Austria. By 2008, a
handful of major sponsors—Vodafone, UEFA, and Nike, to
name three—had emerged to help support the event, and in
tournament literature, there were testimonials from Ringo
Starr, Desmond Tutu, and soccer stars Didier Drogba and
Sir Alex Ferguson citing the importance and worthiness
of the event. This year, 56 teams and over 600 players were
expected to attend, making it the biggest HWC ever.

Australia was a natural location for the tournament, having established one of the most-involved and farthest-reaching homeless soccer programs. Because Melbourne was the centre of these efforts—not to mention the country's most multicultural and freethinking city—it was the organizers' first choice for the event. Local government had also pledged to help partly underwrite the tournament, and a teeming volunteer force had been recruited not weeks after the event was announced.

Melbourne is a city of four million people. When planning it, the city's founders must have gazed upon Victoria's fine coastline—its glittering waters and delicious beaches—before looking inland and deciding that what the city needed, in terms of natural splendour, was more natural splendour. Unlike Vancouver, which depends on its oceanfront but largely forgoes civic beauty, or Hong Kong, where masses scramble over whatever remains of its valley, Melbourne is still a city largely shrouded in green. With the exception of its bohemian enclaves, the gardens and parklands surrounding the Yarra River extend for acres across the city, unifying the water with the land. Every now and then, the green yields to quiet city suburbs and neighbourhoods, but because Australian games—cricket, Aussie rules football, rugby, and, to a lesser extent, soccer—rely on wide, grassy spaces, huge swatches of parkland are never far away, no matter where you are standing. That 90 percent of all Aussies live within 20 minutes of water is often cited as a reason for their longstanding sporting prowess, but having great open spaces on which to wave a cricket bat or punt an oblong football doesn't hurt either.

All of Melbourne's arteries lead to Federation Square, the tournament's official home and site of its three makeshift fields. Sitting across the street from the city's old, butter-scotch-coloured train station at the heart of the city, I thought it seemed like a fine place to stage the tournament. Its modern piazza was terraced with steps that pointed at the city's modest tangle of skyscrapers, as well as St. Paul's Cathedral, its spires poking Victoria's ever-changing skies, where, in the early spring, the sun gave way to clouds in equal measure. Behind the terrace was a large open square bordered by the Australian Racing Museum, the Australian Centre for the Moving Image, and one of the state's national art galleries. The complex had an unfortunate broken-cracker '80s facade—the kind of aesthetic design you'd find on old INXS records—but it was somehow excused by its proximity to the Yarra River, where a long riverside boulevard connected the grounds on which the tournament's three pitches had been raised: two modest courts at the far end of the boulevard (called Birrarung Marr) and another located in the square itself. When I first looked around, handfuls of workers in red vests were fitting together the main field's bleachers, which would rise as two grandstands holding upwards of 3,000 people. It was a neat little bandbox of a park, built to meet the modest demands of four-on-four soccer (the homeless game allowed for a smaller field in consideration of the health and fitness of many of its participants), and its only concession to conventional sportainment was a large video screen blinking above the field. This would have been disheartening were it not for the unusual program being broadcast at the time: the Indonesian national news, live from Jakarta. Along with the Australia's tomato-soup-coloured twenty-dollar bills, the people's island twang, and the moist air currents that carried in from the roaring sea, the broadcast helped clean out all of those hours of air travel, and for the first time, push me into the realm of being away.

There was a symbolic grandeur to staging the event in the fat of the city, especially for the hundreds of athletes who'd spent much of their athletic lives kicking soccer balls across scorched fields, bottle-strewn alleyways, and airless recreational courts. Because the games were held in the square, it was impossible for the thousands of people moving daily through the city's veins to ignore them. The venues matched Mel Young's greater mandate: to show people that homeless men and women were part of the city, too, and instead of making fans drive out of the city to some cold sporting monstrosity located in a low-tax suburb, to bring the athletes of the Homeless World Cup to the fans.

AFTER A FEW days in St. Kilda, Team Canada joined the rest of the players at Melbourne University. The buildings' ivy-covered brown brick walls made it seem as if every important person in Melbourne must have gone there. The grounds were landscaped with palms and jackaroos, and possums and bats filled the trees. This was as close as many of the tournament's players would ever get to post-secondary schooling, although for Team USA's captain, Johnny Figueroa, the setting wasn't unfamiliar. Originally from Honduras, he was once a gangbanger in LA who'd altered his life, enrolling at community college before winning a scholarship to study literature in Rome.

The opening reception took place in a courtyard in front of the Wilson Hall lecture theatre. In the moments before the ceremony proper, something astonishing took place. Teams began strolling en masse into the courtyard wearing matching sweatsuits: the gold Lithuanians, sea-blue Finns, Ghana in black-star jackets, Malawi in watermelon pink, the verdant Mexicans, Zimbabweans sporting gold and black, the red and white Poles, the Dutch tulipped orange, the spangled Americans, the Kiwis in traditional all-black, Norwegians plugged under novelty Viking helmets, the South Africans flashing gold and green, Hong Kong in silver, the Afghanis wearing black jerseys with yellow pant stripes, the Irish painted brightly green, and, finally, the Canadians, who looked resplendent—and hardly ragtag—in their red and white national team colours.

After a few moments, the Poles, who were significantly larger and taller than the other teams, settled against a fence and started singing their team song. Their voices were low and manly, like something born out of a Silesian mine shaft. I pushed my tape recorder into the air to preserve the moment, but before long, the Africans—including a team of small Ugandan women in green shorts wearing dollar-store tiaras—decided that leaving the music to a group of large, clunky white men wouldn't suffice, so, delighted and bemused, they filled the air with competing songs, one or two of their players beating their chests to keep time. The Kenyans produced a large flag, which they used as a canopy, and, across from them, the South Africans ranked into a choir, swayed and hollered at the skies. To my ears, a stranger and more glorious cacophony had not been heard.

"What, you're not singing?" said Willie, the coach of Team Nigeria, outraged that the only music I'd produced was the rhythmic pecking of my pen against paper. Almost immediately, he told me that he possessed three other names: Fatty, Madman, and Chicken Baba. Full-bellied with gleaming

teeth and sunlit eyes, Willie said that he'd earned his nicknames after establishing a tradition of rewarding his team
with a bucket of chicken after every win. "My coaching secret,"
he whispered to me, "is chicken!" I told him that it sounded
like one of the shrewdest managerial techniques I'd heard in
a long time, and he waved his hands in the air, saying, "It's
nothing, and the players will play hard anyway. But, you
know, Nigerians love chicken. I love chicken. Maybe it's a way
for the coach to get some chicken, too, eh?" he said, putting a
finger to his temple.

Surveying the scene in front of him, he said, "You know, if
the whole world was like this tournament, it would be a better place. It's easy to share friendship here—talking, playing,
interacting. At the Homeless World Cup, you are instantly
accepted. When we started in Lagos, nobody wanted to listen
to us, but now we have a full league. We registered over 2,000
players last year. We've helped eight children go to school,
and whenever someone comes to us, we stress the importance of studying. In Africa, people want to put all their eggs
in one basket, but you must get involved in vocational training, no matter what else you are doing. I was a good player on
a professional team in Lagos, but I got injured, and it was the
best thing to happen to me because I went to school. Last year,
two of our players who competed in Copenhagen went to the
sporting institute, and now they are full coaches. This is why
we do what we do, and maybe this is the reason why our players listen to me.

"But, you know," he said, pausing for moment. "Homelessness in Nigeria doesn't necessarily mean not having a home.
Africans know that if you go to a city, even if you don't know
anybody, someone will give you a home. People who are really

homeless are either lunatics or a lazy person who doesn't want to do anything."

Willie excused himself, and I watched him disappear into the courtyard's wild kaleidoscope of sound and colour. At that moment, I noticed that there was one team not singing: the Indians. As it turned out, there were a couple of reasons for this. First, because the team's players came from six Indian states and spoke six different languages, communicating with anyone, even their own teammates, was difficult. Second, many of them had travelled 2,500 km—the equivalent of three full days—by mud-ravaged autorickshaw, rust-bolted train, spit-soldered bus, and bent-bodied car just to reach the team's training headquarters in Nagpur for a two-week session before leaving for Oz. The players from the south had just met the players from the north, and before their trip, the only travel they'd ever done had been out of necessity, compelled by poverty and hardship to leave one slum for another.

The team's coach was a fellow named Abhijeet Barse, who stood a few inches past six feet in height. "Call me Ab," he told me, in a soft, quavering voice. Ab smiled a long, regretful smile when he told me that it had taken the Indians 32 hours to reach Melbourne. They'd been scheduled to fly out of Mumbai just as the city was bombed and were rerouted to Bangkok, only to discover that students had commandeered the airport. Throughout the ordeal, Ab had to try and convince his fragile team that this wasn't a case of bad shit following them around. *This is just the nature of our world*, he told them calmly. *But we have our tickets to Australia. We'll get there. They are expecting us.*

At Indian customs, they were detained for two hours after an immigration officer refused to believe that one of the players' photos was his own. They insisted that it was a white person's photo and that the player had stolen it. After arriving in Sydney, the situation went from bad to worse when they lost a player in the airport, an elfin rickshaw repairman from Ujjain named Sawan Nigam.

Sawan lived and worked in his repair shop, sleeping on a cardboard mat among boxes of engine parts. He spoke no English; nor had he ever been on a plane in his life. Ab privately feared the worst. Still, if this would have sent other teams falling to the mat, the Indian players were used to trouble and having to make unwanted choices. One athlete, Amol Roy, a forward from Assam, had spent most of his life travelling with his family looking for work until, one day, his parents told him that they could no longer support him. *You must leave us. Go. Any life is better than this one.* He hopped off the train that was carrying his family and walked on. It was all he could do to not collapse in despair, but somehow, he kept walking. He walked for days until he found an odd job, then another, then another. Then, one day, he saw the local slum soccer team playing on a dirt patch.

Team India's goaltender—who was known by a single name, Homkant—was the tallest player on the team. He was the son of a poor marginal labourer from a remote village, Ner, which is near Yavatmal in the state of Maharashtra. One year after harvest, farmers started killing themselves. Dozens died, and then a dozen more, until a suicide epidemic consumed the small farming village. Because of these demons, Homkant ran. He kept running until he reached Yavatmal, where the Zopadpatti slum tournament was taking place. Out of this cloud of death, Homkant watched as players young and old kicked a ball around and laughed. Soon, he was playing, too.

Deepak Hoe lived with his mother and eight siblings in a hut in Jharkhand made of wood scraps and discarded metal. When Ab had seen these living conditions first hand, he offered to help Deepak move, but he refused, saying *I have obligation to take care of my family. If I don't take care of them, who will?* For some athletes, coming to live for ten days in Australia would mean swimming in the ocean, eating endless portions of catered food, and meeting people from countries they never knew existed. But for Deepak, the rewards were simpler: a room with a pillow on his bed, floor space without his siblings' arms and legs carpeted below him, a crow landing on the wainscotting of his window, *a window*, bookshelves, and an impressive writing desk, all of which must have looked to Deepak like a palace.

While other teams called their program "Street Soccer," in India, it was "Slum Soccer." The idea for the team started with Ab's 63-year-old father, Vijay, a retired school teacher with a face worthy of a bronzesmith's bust and a Brahman stature that commanded attention. Vijay was the team's manager and a street soccer pioneer, having initiated the program in 2000. "One July day, I was on the way to my duties at the university when the rain started to fall," he remembered. "I was trying to stay dry by standing under a neem tree. The grounds in front of me were filled with water and mud, but there was a group of slum children with no shirts or shoes playing soccer. Everybody else was running to escape the rain, but they didn't care; they kept on playing. But they didn't use a ball. Instead, they were playing with an old cracked bucket. It looked like a few more kicks and it would be ruined, but you knew that even if it fell apart, it wouldn't be enough to keep them from playing. When the rain stopped, I went to my school and found a football, which I gave to them."

After discovering that there was no sporting system in place for underprivileged youth, Vijay set up games for the children against kids from other slums. "There were no rules: no offsides, no shoes, no formality. I just wanted them to play, even if they didn't know anything about football," he said. There was some local news coverage, so interest in the program spread.

The program was wholly financed by Vijay's retirement pension. He purchased all of the balls used by the first handful of teams and bought a local building in Nagpur, home to the team's national program. Still, because of limited resources, the players had to do whatever they could to keep slum soccer alive in their region. An Indian forward named Rajesh had built his own field—the first and only in his village—using borrowed tools and supplies, without any knowledge of horticulture or grounds keeping. He seeded the grass and babied the pitch until it was ready, and what was once a dry, scorched square of nothing was now a field alive with the children of the village.

"There isn't a culture of charity in India like in the United States, so the struggle to keep the program alive is very real," Ab told The New York Times soccer blog. "If it were a homeless cricket team, I would find all the sponsors I would ever need. India has changed a lot, but in some ways not at all. The people in the slums are still forgotten." Ab hoped that the success of their program in tournaments like the HWC could help change this attitude. Of Team India's six players, three had earned coaching licences and were working in Indian schools, while two were employed by slum soccer and attending college.

The establishment of sporting programs in India has always been a difficult endeavour. It's long been a riddle why

India—a nation of one billion people, many of them sports-men—has failed to climb into the world's elite athletic ranks, although crippling bureaucracy and the lack of infrastructure are often cited as two of the reasons. A few months before the HWC, the 2008 Summer Olympics yielded one of India's most surprising athletic triumphs when Abhinav Bindra, a 25-year-old computer-game company executive, won a gold medal in the 10-metre air rifle competition. Bindra, who hails from Chandigarh in the north, was widely celebrated for his rare and remarkable achievement (it was India's first gold medal since 1980). He was awarded 2.5 million rupees ($59,000 dollars US) by the Board of Control for Cricket, and the minister of railways gave him a lifetime rail pass in an air-conditioned car.

While Indians play a multitude of indigenous games, such as kabbadi and badminton, and colonial sports, such as polo, one has to travel great distances not to see a soccer ball being kicked about. Still, the Indian national soccer team has for-ever ranked in the low 90s despite a citizenry deeply attuned to the game. In the early part of this century, the Indians were managed by an Englishman of Greek extraction, Ste-phen Constantine, who immediately improved the team's performance by drafting men and boys from all regions of the subcontinent. Constantine told the football magazine *When Saturday Comes* that "when I arrived, there was a regional divide, with the Calcutta boys in one camp and the Bombay boys in another. I insisted on mixing it up [so that] we did everything together. A lot of things needed shaking up. There was also a culture of complacency. Once you were in the squad, you were safe for five years. I wasn't [reluctant] to drop some of the old guard and pick 17-year-olds if they were good enough."

Constantine wrote in an email that "for a long time, only boys of high caste who lived in West Bengal were considered worthy to participate in the national team program. Organizers had traditionally ignored most of the country, choosing instead to give spots to players from wealthy families." One of the first things he did was scour the slums of Calcutta, finding skilled players among the poor enclaves of the city.

Constantine left the program in 2005, but where his work ended, Ab and Vijay's began. "We want to decentralize soccer," Ab said, "bringing it to all of the regions. We have six states represented on our team, but we want to reach out to create a true national organization for boys of every stripe." The country's national homeless tournament, held in Nagpur, bore this out, featuring teams from Maharashtra, Uttarakhand, Bihar, Gujarat, Vidarbha, Chhattisgarh, Madhya Pradesh, and Jammu and Kashmir.

The Wilson Hall reception should have been a kind of victory lap for India's management and players. Instead, the team grew melancholy while drinking watermelon and ginger punch—handed to them in plastic champagne flutes by waiters in red vests, no less—and fretting about their missing teammate. Then, as the other teams mixed about the courtyard, which became more crowded still with the arrival of seven accredited international documentary crews, a tiny figure with a thin moustache and small, unwavering eyes—the only person in the crowd not wearing a team uniform—wandered through the masses: Sawan Nigam, the missing player. The Indians rejoiced but fell short of breaking into song. Still, the giddy relief in their voices was a kind of music all the same.

THE ATHLETES WERE called into Wilson Hall for the opening ceremonies and team draw. A handful of local emissar-
ies spoke from a low-lit stage, then a group of Aboriginal
musicians performed a few traditional songs on didgeridoo,
once called tree-tremblers by the Aussie musical parodist
Rolf Harris, or *didgeridon'ts* by a drummer friend of mine. A
young Turkish émigré named Oz—Canada's tournament liaison—rolled his eyes during much of the presentation. After
the tree-tremblers finished, I asked him if organizers also
planned on serving us shrimp-on-the-barbie. He scoffed:
"Man, I've never had shrimp-on-the-barbie in my life. These
are things that Australians get tourists to do so we don't have
to do them ourselves."

The room was mostly quiet when Mel Young, the HWC's
éminence grise, addressed the players, telling them that
"the flat, simple road goes nowhere, but climbing a mountain means there's always something ahead." Everyone was
hushed throughout these words except the Kenyans, who'd
removed their shoes and were sitting in the balcony directly
behind Team Canada. They never stopped talking—a low,
sonorous rumble that roiled across the seats, one player telling an excited story, then another, then another. Nobody
had the nerve to hush them, and the teams who were sitting around us—the Finns, Mexicans, Russians, and Portu-
guese—seemed amused by this lack of formal observance.
Still, no one was more pleased than Billy. Team Canada's
motormouth was off the hook.

During the tournament draw, cheers erupted whenever a
country's name was announced. After organizers had seeded
all 54 teams—only two clubs, from Croatia and Slovenia, had
failed to make the trip—players returned to the courtyard

to study the draw card. Canada was grouped with two powerhouses (Ghana and Russia), one contender (the Netherlands), and two relative minnows (Cambodia and Sierra Leone). It wasn't the greatest draw, but it wasn't the Group of Death, either, which had Afghanistan, Scotland, Zimbabwe, and Mexico playing together. Paul and Cris announced that the team's opening game would be against the Dutch in two days, allowing the players some time to shake the jet lag out of their heads and bodies.

The members of Team Canada adjourned almost immediately to their rooms. When Paul asked Jerry why he was leaving so early, he joked, "I've got a bottle of vodka to take care of." I implored Billy to stay and meet some of the other competing players with me, but he waved his hand and said, "No, man, I've got to get straight back to my room. I mean, it's not gonna decorate itself, you know?"

Krystal was too sick with excitement to hang around. The bewildered look on her face suggested a person who'd fallen through a fissure in life only to land in the world's forgiving loam, surrounded by people she'd read about in public school textbooks and from places she never knew existed. As she walked out of the hall, a few of the African men called to her—some wolf-whistled, some made bird sounds and waved their arms—but Krystal kept her head down and kept walking. Before leaving the courtyard, she was approached by a Nigerian woman named Chi Chi, who wore red braids and long beaded loops hanging around her neck and wrists. Krystal stopped and extended her hand. Chi Chi spoke in a shy, careful way, and Krystal listened. After a moment, Krystal tipped back on her heels and laughed, and before parting ways, she put her hand on her African friend's shoulder and wished her good luck in the tournament. Chi Chi turned smiling and returned to her team, and Krystal headed back to the dorm, bowing her head and shaking it slightly, as if rattling her jigsaw of thoughts would find her back in Regent Park. But she was nowhere other than very far from home.

6

500

MILES

THE OFFICIAL OPENING of the HWC began the next day with a parade down Collins and Swanston streets to Federation Square. The buses were late leaving the campus for the city because no one could find the Austrians. Team Canada sat in silence waiting on its coach without a clue as to what might happen next. But this silence was soon broken by the team from Zimbabwe, who arrived in a clapping procession of swaying backs and shoulders dressed in black, gold, and green track suits and singing, just as they'd done in the courtyard the day before. They sang coming up the steps; they sang strutting down the aisle; and they sang as they settled into the back of the bus. The only Zimbabwean not singing was their manager, Thomas, a sloe-eyed young man wearing a baseball cap who sat between the players and nodded his head appreciatively.

Thomas joined Team Canada at the front of the bus. When I asked him how things were going at home, he replied in a soft whisper that swam beneath the team's music, forcing me to ask him again. When I finally heard him, I almost wished I hadn't asked: "Things are very, very bad in my country," he said. "Right now, you see, there are fires of rage in Zimbabwe."

Through corporate donations and a central fund, the Homeless World Cup had provided for the African teams' journey to Oz. Although most of the visiting teams experienced culture shock, it was probably most extreme for the Zimbabweans, who came from a place where, Thomas told us, "there is no food, only economic terrorism. It is terrible and people are starving. The government refuses to let the NGOs go to where the deep poverty is, which is 80 percent of the country, a country where the military burns houses and where, many years ago, Operation Restore Order put my family into one camp, then another, then another. Eight years of my life, gone."

While the players clapped and stomped and shouted *Ohhhh-Ya!* and *HumbabaHumbabaHumbabaAye!* Thomas leaned in and continued: "When I was a child, my parents couldn't afford to stay in proper housing, so we went to a camp. We were there for six months until this man—a politician—gave up his farm, turning it into a place for squatters, where we lived and worked freely. But because he'd democraticized his land, the government noticed him and grew jealous, saying that it couldn't be a residential place. They said that no man would be allowed to prove the ruling party wrong, so they sent in the police and the army with live ammunition and they dismantled the farm, burning it, turning everything red with flames. We were forced into the streets until election time, at which point the government found the squatters a new place, or so we thought. They took us there, our new homes, but only if we supported the ruling party. This was not possible so they burned it before our very eyes, sending us to another camp, then another, and another, and, well, you know the story. But that's when I met someone. He was an Australian United Nations communications officer who worked alongside UNICEF. A good man."

Outside, the bus must have looked like a child's enormous windup toy as it rocked with the teams' songs. But inside, Thomas's sorrowful voice thrummed across the players' singing like a cello bowed between two low notes played at the top of the neck. "I'd always wanted to be a doctor," he said, "and I told this to the man from UNICEF. He asked me to be realistic and to formulate a plan, and so I did, envisioning a kind of play therapy for the children. In Zimbabwe, soccer is played everywhere despite the tornado of war; it's played in empty swimming pools, in car parks, in squatters' camps, and it's inexpensive, so that became my plan, to motivate the youth through soccer so that they could have some freedom of the soul, some motivation in these terrible circumstances. In Cape Town, at the Homeless World Cup, one of our players met someone who helped him go to school. He is studying accounting now and has a new life. Another person—a drug addict whose family and home were destroyed by the government—joined our program and is now the coach of the Zimbabwean national team. As for the rest of us, we are here, in Australia, playing soccer. I cannot predict the future, but I know that anything is possible, even when everything else seems impossible. We are living proof of this simply because, despite everything, we are here."

After Thomas returned to his team, the Canadian players grew quiet, drowned in thought. It was easy, perhaps, to assume what they were thinking: *My life is what it is. But at least my neighbourhood's not on fire. At least no one's trying to gun me down for 20 cents in my pocket.* After a few moments, Krystal broke the silence, saying: "We should be singing something, too. What about that song, 'And I could walk 500 miles?' That's Canadian, right?"

"It's Scottish," I told her. "The Proclaimers. From Scotland."

"We could do it anyway," she said.

"How about 'Souvlaki'?" suggested Billy, drawing puzzled looks.

"That's a song?" asked Cris.

"A song, a food. Whatever," he said, waving his hand.

Krystal said: "Next year, we need a team song, okay?"

Paul turned to me, "Dave could write one."

"On second thought, I think one of The Proclaimers' aunts lives in Toronto. I'm pretty sure that qualifies as CanCon," I said.

Just then, the Zimbabweans' jukebox yielded a familiar chant—"*Boombaye! Boombaya!*"—Eric's notorious goal-crease slogan.

"Hey, that's what Eric says!" said Krystal, pointing to the back of the bus.

"Man, Eric's here after all," added Billy, clapping his hands.

If Team Canada had no tournament song, at least it had its crackhead goalie's anthem channelled through the Zimbabwean player's hymn. It was certainly more appropriate than anything by The Proclaimers.

The Austrians eventually appeared, and the procession of buses chugged to life. If the sight of a dozen coaches rambling into downtown wouldn't have stirred the locals, the sight of the athletes did, arriving at midday and surprising the heart of the city with an explosion of bodies and voices. If one of the main issues of homelessness was invisibility, the parade established that, for the next week anyway, the athletes of the 2008 HWC would not walk in shadows.

At first, the scene looked like a rogue's operative, transforming the city into something out of a Lionel Bart musical imagined by Tom Waits. There was more singing as teams chanted behind the sound of a roving jazz octet, who played "Tequila," as a way of toasting the athletes. The Malawians herded a group of children into a loose circle and showed them quick-footed African dances with a small, yellow soccer ball bouncing at its epicentre. The long-haired Chileans— who were trailed all tournament by a procession of pretty young women—sang "Ole/Ole/Ole!/Chil-e/Chil-e!" with arms entwined, and the Cambodians stood in the middle of the street quietly humming what I assumed was their national anthem. The Irish and Scottish, for their part, barked taunts at the English, who laughed and showed them the reverse side of two fingers widened into a V. Those working in Melbourne's surrounding commercial district wandered out of their shops as if drawn to a holiday celebration they hadn't known existed. Before long, the sidewalks were silly with people as organizers tried grouping the teams into alphabetical order. Then someone barked into a bullhorn and the parade started moving in earnest.

Each team was joined by a group of local school children chosen to march at the head of the procession. At first, Team Canada seemed encumbered by their longstanding tradition of trying to be heard above the fray while being reluctant to become part of the fray itself. Were this a parade of hockey players, the athletes might have been more voluble and confident, but as minnows in a tournament populated with famous soccer-playing nations, it was hard for them to summon any measure of braggadocio. The players were grateful and relieved, then, when the school children took up a chant of "Ca-na-da," inspiring someone from the crowd to shout above the din: "Better than the USA!" Having spent years on stage trying to be heard above great volumes, I blurted "Eh!" at the end of the chant's measure. The players took up this call and response with gusto as the procession sloped towards the main stadium.

The athletes soon filled the heart of the thoroughfare, pushing everyone else to the margins of the street. Along the route, parade-goers raised their hands to high-five the players, and almost every player was quick to return the touch. The moment was fat with irony. Having spent years being ignored or sneered at by passersby—to say nothing of suffering cruelty, beatings and, for those who weren't here, death, at the hands of police, miscreants, and thugs—the homeless were now being cheered in the fullness of the Australian sunshine. To move alongside them was to swim in the butterscotch of the moment, the players behaving as if loosed from years of hardship and social poison.

Ahead of the Canadians marched Team Belgium, with whom they shared a university dorm. One of the first things the Belgians had done after finding their rooms was hang their country's flag on a doorway through which their floormates were required to pass. This scratched the Canadians' competitive itch and, for a moment, gave them reason to cheer against their floormates. But like Team Canada, the

Belgians had suffered through hard times while trying to get to Melbourne. Two of their players had been refused entry to Australia only weeks before the tournament as a result of crimes that had occurred long ago. Their manager, a dread-locked woman named Merje, hung her head when describing how counsellors had cried while breaking the news to their players, devastated that hardline Australian immigration authorities could not be swayed (HWC organizers had tried to pull some strings, but it was impossible for them to save every player who'd been red flagged). Even worse, she said, was that when organizers called home to give updates on the team's progress, the counsellors reported that the rejected players were crestfallen, and some of them had started using again.

While many teams participating in the HWC possessed a certain athletic verisimilitude—the Irish, for instance, looked like long distance runners; the Ghanaians were sinewy and taut-bodied; and the French were typically handsome and strong—the Belgians gave the appearance of concession-aires rather than competitors. They were of two distinct body types: round and soft, or skinny and haggard-looking. More than any other team, they hid nothing of their essence. For a lot of tournament players, being around a group of athletes was nothing new, but to the Belgians, it was all new. They marched reluctantly, distrustful of the crowd and bewildered by the daylight. They were like the cast of *One Flew Over the Cuckoo's Nest*, freed from their psych ward, astonished at having been released from the burden of their lives.

Diana Loewen was Belgium's lone female player, a spiky-haired, thick-trunked woman who'd only just left the streets. At first, she'd lived with her grandmother, but she had recently found an apartment with the help of Antwerp's social assistance program.

"Life on the Antwerp streets is very hard," she told me, pulling on a smoke. "People look at you like you're scum, but they don't know how tough it is. The hardest part is having nothing. You see people out shopping, riding in nice cars on their way home. You fantasize about their lives, but when you come out of that fantasy, you're still on the streets, sleeping in the metro, under bridges, wherever you can. It's dangerous because of the gangs, and while the police try to control them, they don't help you either. They swarm you and tell you to go away, call you a disgrace, a loser, a junkie. But my problem was never drugs. I had money problems, and Antwerp is an expensive city. It's a mean city, too. People pretend to give you money, then they spit at you." She looked over the sea of bodies. "This parade is great, because, for once in my life people aren't yelling at me or giving me the finger. I feel almost normal."

There was another Belgian player, a fellow named Eric, who was chosen to replace one of the team's four banished players. Eric had never played a minute of soccer in his life. He was tall and overweight and moved with a kind of slow clunkiness, stomping up and down the court before eventually coming to rest, red-faced and wheezing.

"My problem started with finance," he said, as he waved a small Belgian flag. "I took a loan with my girlfriend, and when we broke up, I was forced to pay for it myself. I also had problems at work, where the boss was ripping me off, and because I wasn't making a decent wage, I had to give up my apartment. I don't drink, I don't do drugs, and I don't have a criminal record, but I had to move into a shelter, a place I never thought I'd be. In the shelter, I saw people who'd suffered a lot worse than me. It helped me realize that I should be happy in my situation. I had a lot of time to think about my life, about everything. Eventually, my sister took me in, giving me a spare room in her house, and, just this summer, I got my own apartment. When I first saw it, it was empty, but it was one of the most beautiful things I've ever seen. I had a very bad youth, living with a very aggressive father and a mother who was crazy, and who's in a psychiatric ward she will probably never leave. In this sense, I'd never had a proper home. I got married much too young, at 19, because my first wife was pregnant. Every decision I made was a bad one, and before I got my own place, I was ashamed of my life. But my house now is always clean. I do the dishes; I sweep all of the time.

"Pride," he said, as the parade rolled forward to the main stadium. "It's about finding pride in your life. If I could pass on anything, it's that you don't have to be a drug addict to live on the streets. Take it from me. It can happen to absolutely anyone."

The procession gained momentum as it neared the Federation Square pitch, which many of the players were now seeing for the first time. Flags of competing nations ringed the field, and an enormous vinyl billboard of a player kicking a ball in mid-flight hung behind the grandstand. Approaching the stadium, you could hear the rumble of fans—thousands had gathered to await the tournament's ceremonial first match between Australia and Afghanistan—as well as the voice of an announcer shouting into a Tannoy. Teams were drawn into a crowded area behind the pitch before being called, one at a time, into the tiny stadium. When it was Canada's turn, Krystal, Jerry, Juventus, and Billy jogged across the field's dark rubber waving to the crowd. Watching them from the sidelines and seeing their faces, you got the sense that if they were to board a plane that night and return home, something about this trip would have already been fulfilling. For them, and for every other player, a kind of victory had been achieved before they'd kicked a single ball.

The last team to enter the stadium was Zimbabwe, still singing. Thomas trailed the players, moving hands-in-pockets at the back of their procession. At one point, he raised his eyes to the crowd, and I looked for that glint of wonder and amazement that had possessed the rest of the athletic body. But it was impossible to find. Still, watching him and his players stride across the openness of the court, I wouldn't have guessed that by tournament's end, the entire team from Zimbabwe would disappear from sight, seeking political asylum in Oz.

7

DOVE

TEAM CANADA'S FIRST day of competition began atop a hill overlooking Birrarung Marr. Organizers had assembled an inflatable red practice pitch that looked like a child's enormous jumping castle. Elevated above the grounds, the players found that their sightline was even with a wall of city buildings that rose behind the hill, facing the great bold letters of the HERALD SUN, a venerable Melbourne press. Even though they were anxious to kick the ball around after days spent doing everything but playing, Billy and Krystal turned for a moment towards the city, looking like two mountaineers who had just conquered a once indomitable rock face.

The players leapt over the wide borders of the inflatable field to find a mesh bag of soccer balls emptied onto the ground, which was parched and pebbled after years of repeated drought. Paul and Cristian tried to organize a series of passing and shooting drills, a test of the players' ability after twenty hours of travel followed by two days in St. Kilda. Balls sprayed around the court as if burst from a bingo popper, and while it became apparent that the transcontinental journey hadn't robbed the Canadians of their skills, the nets were empty even though not a single repellent force stood in the way of their boots of glory.

This changed, however, once Paul appeared with the team's substitute goaltender, a fellow named David from Port Glasgow, Scotland. When the Canadians first saw him, he was dressed in black and slugging up the hill as if steeling his body against the advance of an unseen predator. If you didn't look directly at his hands—which were gnawed and crudely tattooed at the knuckles—you might have thought they were balled into fists, given his tightened haunch and slow, suspicious pace. He had barbed-wire eyes and a small, bulldog's nose, and his rough, time-scribbled face narrated a journey of endless hardship. He squinted at the sun as if trying to pinch the brightness of the horizon into dust, and his teeth forever clenched a burning cigarette, which left a trail of blue smoke behind him as he walked towards his new teammates.

"This is David, our goalkeeper," said Cris, with appropriate formality.

David butted out his smoke under the heel of a boot.

"Caul me Dove," he said, in a deep molasses brogue. "They been caulin' me Dove evah since I was sayven."

Dove's legs were also tattooed. So were his arms and his chest. They weren't the kind of drawings worn by hipsters or the result of the Best Ever Kegger. They looked like they'd been applied by a razor or penknife in a cold cement cell, a deckhand's quarters, or the backroom of a storefront long ago boarded up on a deserted street. Even though Team Canada's players had all seen their share of shit and misery, the lingering effects were mostly mental. But Dove's scarred and deeply grooved face seemed imprinted with the suffering of his former life.

Dove arrived in Melbourne having recovered from a litany of abuses. He'd grown up poor in a rough city corridor, where his father had taught him how to box. He'd enlisted in the Scottish ranks of the British Army, but the army provided no escape from the streets. He was shipped to Belfast, Northern Ireland, where officers demanded that he patrol Falls Road in the heart of the Catholic powder keg. He witnessed endless violence and bombings. He suffered hatred and mistrust among people for whom his loyalties were divided; as a Scotsman living under British rule, he sympathized with the Irish, but he was also loyal to the British army. The conflict ate him up. He walked through streets of fire, among burnt buses and bodies flung across a blood-strewn roundabout. If the dangers of home had produced only occasional violence, in Belfast it was unrelenting. The comfort and security of a regimental life yielded only chaos and more horror.

One evening, Dove got drunk—*soldier* drunk—with his fellow troops in a bar in Cyprus. Being an accomplished boxer meant that while friends revered him, he was almost always challenged by others. *You're not so fookin' tough. Look at you, ya oogly bastard. That gob of yours has taken a fair bit of poundin', eh?* Twisted by war and savaged by authoritarian abuse, Dove rose to nearly everyone's bait. Some paid the price; some didn't. And some paid a lot worse than others.

The victim was a young RAF pilot. He was 22, give or take a year. The pilot was drunk, brave, and foolish. Perhaps he was poor, like Dove, or perhaps not. *A pilot.* Flight academy. Straight chin, fine hands. British forces. *Imperialist coonts.* "The poor, poor boy," repeated Dove as he told the story. "It was tarrible, what happened. The poor boy lost his life."

Dove was discharged from the army. There was no trial, no jail time. He was sent home, back to Port Glasgow. The only people who understood him were those who'd also killed. "I was surrounded by death. Death up here, death down there," said Dove, passing his ravaged hands over his face, chest, and stomach. "The only thing left for me to do was join the trade," he said, referring to Scotland's raging heroin industry. "I got good at it," he said, with a trace of pride. "Made tons of money. Lived large, you know? Like nayver before, really. 'Course I got addicted and that brought the whole friggin' house down."

Four times, Dove tried to kill himself. Drugs pulled him into an obsolescence of terror, pain, and depression. "I tried doing it every which way," he said, "but I wasn't even very good at that. This only made it worse. Then, one day, I was hanging a noose around the ceiling pipe in my room. I was ready. It was time. But just as I was about to go, my son walked in. He was fifteen years old. And that's when I said, 'No. This is it. This is the end, right here.'"

In recovery, Dove travelled the world, telling his story at Alcoholics Anonymous conventions and then joining the Scottish team. Stepping into the goal for Canada for the first time, he spat into his gloves and slapped away a few volleys before roaring at his new teammates:

"Shoot it hairder, lads! C'mon. Shoot it *hairder!!*"

AFTER PRACTICE, the team marched down the hill towards the river pitches. One minute, the sun burned hot; the next, a flight of clouds arrived to soften the heat. The courts backed onto one another and were separated by a tented area with little rooms that looked like a makeshift triage unit (there was one of those, too, rooted alongside the catering tent located on the rooftop of a nearby parking garage). The scene backstage was a collision of nations: teams who'd just played, were about to play, and were arriving to play next. This global sporting carnival was played out to the sounds of an announcer shouting into a microphone and the music of Oasis, AC/DC, and Queen—or at least a chorus from one song, then a verse from the other—blaring from the court's speakers.

Canada collected in one of these rooms, where the players fell silent. Krystal plugged in her earphones and paced around, shaking her arms loose and occasionally staring at the ceiling. Every now and then, she sang a few words to whatever song she was listening to, then hopped up and down on the spot, throwing her head back and forth while preparing to meet the demands of whatever lay ahead.

The HWC soccer courts were made of black rubber, which absorbed the heat and tended to catch the shoe. The ball itself was almost sticky against the field, more so on days when the sun was at its boldest. The nets were recessed into the field's framing, and at times, the goaltenders looked like the guardians of a very small garage. The dimensions of the field were 16 metres by 22 metres: tiny parks that preserved the fast pace of the game and ensured that the physically untuned homeless athlete would not be required to run miles for the ball, which, in the four-on-four street soccer game, ping-ponged off waist-high boards and occasionally jumped like a house pet in the tight corners of the field.

Over the years, street soccer—or homeless soccer; organizers waffled about what exactly to call the game—had gone through a handful of rule changes. One of the more substantial changes was the three-on-two rule. Like a lot of modern sporting inventions—baseball's designated hitter, hockey's shootout, basketball's three-pointer—the three-on-two rule was employed to ramp up scoring, although why the degree or amount of scoring should matter in a goodwill event was not clear. (When I raised this issue with Lawrence Cann, he suggested, flatly, "At the end of the day, it's a soccer tournament. Teams come here to win.") The three-on-two rule required that one player per team remain in the offensive zone at all times, never crossing the centre line. This rule ensured two things: one, teams had to play three men players back at all times and could not "trap" other teams, and two, there were always three players outnumbering two in the offensive zone. It partly meant that, in blow-out games, the lone offensive player for the losing team had little to do, and whenever there was a disparity in talent—which there was when pretty much every poor-to-middling team played Ghana, Afghanistan, Russia, Ireland, and others—the scores were often inflated and unflattering to both sides.

Canada was eventually called to the court. They warmed up opposite the Dutch, who stole furtive glances down the pitch. The Canadian team was also supplemented by an Australian reserve, a six-foot-three defender named Pommie, who was covered head to toe in Tensor bandages, his arms and legs wrapped to protect injuries that he'd suffered in training sessions leading up to the tournament.

After a while, the sides were ordered to the centre line for the playing of their national anthems. Paul waved for me to join them, and I allowed myself the moment. A wonky high-school orchestra's recording of "O Canada" came over the speakers as we stood at mid-court in front of a few hundred fans gathered in the bleachers. For me, the music evoked the dusty winter warmth of a small classroom, a music instructor in a plaid sweater and pleated corduroys furiously waving a baton. What the song evoked for the others, however, I couldn't be sure. Billy, as an occasional alternate for Team Canada in the '80s, had heard the anthem played at games many times before. Once, he'd heard it while standing mid-field in Azteca Stadium in Mexico City. When I asked him what it had been like to play in the famous park, known as "the cauldron," he reared back his head and said, incredulously: "What was it like? What was it *like*? I puked. That's what it was like."

The Canadians sang along with their anthem, chins tilted to the skies. At the far end of the line, Dove did too, if a few beats behind the rest, shadowing the words he was hearing for the first time. When the song ended, the referee—a tall, cadaverous gentleman dressed in black—called Krystal, Billy, and Jerry into position (Juventus and Pommie would start on the sidelines), then tweeted his whistle as the ball was booted into play.

The game started with a flurry of nervous energy—chests heaving, arms and ankles swinging. The wildly orange sweaters of the Dutchmen swirled against the black rubber of the pitch and, for the first few minutes, the Canadians looked like Keystone Kops chasing after Halloween truants. From the beginning, the Dutch seemed fitter, better, and more organized, so it was no surprise when they opened the scoring with four quick goals, blasting Dove with shots from every corner of the field. Their team had a distinct advantage over the Canadians, possessing twice the number of players on their roster, which they'd assembled after a series of national playdowns featuring a dozen homeless soccer teams from a dozen cities. There were no Tensor-wrapped Pommies or overweight seat-cushion salesmen on the Dutch team, either; only swift-footed Edgar Davids doppelgangers who bumped the score to 5–0 before Canada made its first substitution: Juventus for Krystal. Krystal came to the bench, grabbed a water bottle, and then lowered her head as she emptied it across her shoulders and neck. With beads of water dripping from her brow, she closed her eyes and inhaled deeply before staring back at the field and shouting with the full force of her shoulders:

"C'mon Canadaaaaaaaaa!!!"

Despite the substitution, the Dutch kept shooting. This might have disheartened lesser competitors, but Dove faced each shot as if he welcomed the ball's rough hide, punching away volleys like a child batting his birthday balloons. Whenever he rolled across the crease to capture a ball, he came up with his teeth to the grill, devouring every delicious second of action, as if getting hit with cannon fire was a gift. It was the kind of reaction one might have expected from someone who'd conquered the terrible ravages of his life, and while falling behind 7–0 to the Netherlands probably wasn't the greatest start to his tournament, considering all that had happened in Dove's life, it also sort of was. Even in lopsided drubbings like these, at least he was playing.

Juventus ran around the field like a dog loosed from its chain, his pompadour of hair pitching from side to side. Almost instantly, he flung himself into the fray in an attempt to take the ball from one of the tall Dutch forwards. But he ended up planting his knee in the unforgiving rubber and twisting it. Juve felt a shudder of pain in his kneecap, and a sharp popping sound could be heard from the sidelines. He slumped to the turf and rubbed his leg. Juve's implacable repose soon erupted into grief and disappointment as he drew himself up from the grounds and limped in slow, agonizing steps to the sidelines. Cristian was hopeful that his injury would be the kind that only needed to loosen before it healed, but when Juve stopped walking, leaned against the wall along the sidelines, and stood there groaning, the coaches and players knew to expect the worst.

The bad news didn't end there. Early in the second half, Dove lunged after a rolling ball, trapped it heroically, then lay prone in the goalmouth holding his thigh. His hard expression remained, but, as he clambered to his feet, his body was tilted to one side as if favouring his right leg. Cristian yelled at him, asking if he was okay, but Dove refused to ask for time. The shots kept coming, and almost every one of them was a goal. Cris yelled at him again, but Dove simply looked away and held up the flat of his gloves, continuing to play even though he'd stretched a groin, ending his tournament in red and white.

At game's end, the bedraggled Canadians turned to comfort their goalie. "Way to go out there, Doug," said Billy. No one had the energy to correct him. Out of the stands came a cheer—"Ca-na-da!"—and when the players looked up from their post game huddle, they saw that it was their floormates, the Belgians, lending their support. A while later, it was discovered that Juventus had suffered the worst possible kind of leg injury: a torn ligament in his knee. Over the next few days, he would disappear as mysteriously as he had arrived. His tournament was over, but for the rest of the team, it had only just begun.

8

VANNIE
AND THE
MOUNTAIN
LIONS

HAVING ALREADY LOST two players, Paul
was required to revisit the organizing committee and request a new pair of substitutes. "Sometimes I
think that I've had just about enough of this," he said as he
crossed the grounds, sounding the social worker's lament.
Even though he was hanging out in a beautiful city on the
other side of the world—he'd used his vacation time from
work to come to the tournament—it was still his responsibility to manage people who had trouble managing themselves.
That he was already feeling taxed didn't bode well for the
duration of the event.

Paul's request yielded a new pair of Australian reserves
for Canada's next game versus Sierra Leone. One was another
boxer, a 28-eight-year-old half-Aboriginal, half-Italian wel-
terweight named P.J., whose thick New South Wales accent
made him sound as if he were chewing on a hunk of meat.

Standing six feet tall, with short dark hair and a nose damaged by a flurry of left hooks, P.J. jumped around as if he were standing on hot coals. He bobbed up and down when he spoke, and when I first encountered him in the athlete's courtyard at the university, I thought he was high. But he was just naturally jumpy. P.J. provided Team Canada with a measure of breathless energy, but this restlessness also proved to be his athletic shortcoming. During games, he chased multiple players at once and tried to cover both ends of the court at the same time.

The first thing P.J. told his new teammates was that he'd recently won a cheesecake-making contest. It was probably the last thing they expected to hear from a homeless prizefighter. Billy rubbed his belly as he listened to P.J. describe how he made his ribbon-winning macadamia-nut crust, stressing the importance of including a strange indigenous fruit. "A cross between a papaya and a guava," said P.J., "and the cheesecake's pièce de résistance." While the players stood on the riverside boulevard imagining the taste of P.J.'s confection, he talked about other aspects of his life, too. Like how he'd been left for dead by his parents and had tried taking his life several times.

"I was about five years old when I was taken away from my mom," he said. "My nonna helped me get away from her; she knew what was going on. I was put in a home for about five years in Victoria. When my brother and I were in care, we had the longest stay of any of the home's orphans. No one wanted us. We were considered damaged goods, and we'd watch other kids walk out the door, but we were always left behind. One day, we were on the local news and in the newspapers, and this helped find us a family. We were thrilled, but what we didn't know was that they had a gay son, and all kinds of terrible things happened to us while we lived there. This went on for about a year or so. The welfare people found out about it and we were put back in the home again before being sent to a different family, who beat us, hit us, whenever they felt like it for four years. One day after school, I took two biscuits out of a cookie jar and they beat me with jumper cables. Because we lived on a vineyard, our mother would go out, grab a cane off the vine, and whale on us. One night, I remember my brother screaming for help. We were both young and helpless, and no one could do anything about it.

"Because of all of that stuff, I got post-traumatic stress. I ran away when I was 16, lived for 12 years on the street. Sometimes, I'd get flashbacks. I'd run down the street screaming because I thought that people were following me. I took medication—antipsychotics—but they only worked so well. One night, my partner tried to wake me and, when I woke up, I reached for her throat. I nearly killed her, choking her in bed because I thought my mother was trying to get me. I couldn't go outside; couldn't be in daylight. I tried to take my life several times, had cuts on my arms after trying to kill myself.

"One night, I was with my daughter's mother. She told me that she didn't love me; that she wanted to go back to her old boyfriend. I went straight to a hotel, looked out the window for about six hours, and thought fuck it, that's it, I'm gonna jump. I was standing out there on the ledge when these lights appeared, the lights of a cop car. They yelled up at me, *What're you doing, man? C'mon down, son.* I told them, *Fuck you, fuck everything; fuck this world and everything about it. I wanna fuckin' die. Leave me alone.* But they grabbed me and took me to the hospital. I got better, but that didn't stop me from wanting to kill myself. Still, every time I tried, someone or something was there to prevent it from happening. Finally, I thought, I guess someone is trying to tell me something here. If I was supposed to die, I should have been dead by now. I'm a Christian guy, so I thought it was maybe Christ telling me that there was something he wanted me to do. I didn't know what that was, but it had to be something. Now, when anyone asks if I'm a survivor, I say *yes. I'm proud of it. I may not have done much, but I've done this.* And I'm here to play. When I'm playing soccer, I've got fresh air coming at me. If I'm kicking a ball, I'm not hurting anyone. Playing sports, you don't think about negative things; it's a way of keeping those devils and demons at bay. On the field, they can't get me, no matter what happens in the game. When my nonna passed away, the last thing she wanted in her life was to see my brother, who'd run away. She never ended up seeing him, but I think she's here," he said, patting his shoulder. "Right here, watching me."

BEFORE THE GAME against Sierra Leone, I found Juve sitting on a chair smoking outside the rooftop dining area. He lifted a hand to wave at me, his knee shrouded in bandages and a bag of ice. Juve groused about not starting in Krystal's place and how the team hadn't discussed strategy or the nature of the starting lineup before the game. Because of the team's impossibly limited training time, I offered that it was all Paul and Cris could do just to field a team, let alone assemble one that was as well-organized as the others. But Juventus scoffed: "I am not upset about the pain or the injury—for the things I've seen in my life, this is nothing—but, as a football decision, not starting me was wrong. I know football. I know football strategy, and that was not good strategy. Every team starts with the three best players, but Cristian put Krystal at forward. This is nothing against Krystal, but really, you see how I play. You know what I can do. Why didn't Cristian put me in to start? I came off the bench and I was cold. It should have been me, not that Greek guy, or that other guy." I suggested that it was endemic of the thrown-together lineup that Juve didn't know either of Billy or Jerry's names, but he said, "names mean nothing to me. Football. Football is what matters to me. And that was not good football."

TEAM CANADA'S NEW goaltender was a frail Vietnamese refugee named Vannie. According to those who knew him, Vannie had a mild intellectual disability. He was fairly new to the Australian street soccer program, too, having recently discovered the game. When Vannie first showed up for practice in Melbourne, he sat for two weeks in the corner of the gym with his legs drawn to his stomach, too afraid or uncertain to participate. He rarely spoke, and when he did, he refused to talk about his life back in Vietnam. But eventually, he was coaxed to the field. George Halkias, Australia's coach, said that if not for the team's weekly practices, there was no telling where Vannie would be in his life. He'd come so far over the last year that he was awarded a coach's citation for his achievements. While sports often provide the only means of escape and self-expression for professional athletes, few players had been as close to dissolution as Vannie was before he found soccer.

After Billy saw Vannie warm up in the crease, he turned to me and said, "We're fucked." Cristian, who was standing next to him along the sidelines, told him, "I heard he played for some team somewhere."

"Yeah, maybe a women's team," said Billy, jogging onto the court. "I just hope I don't hurt the guy," he added, lofting a soft shot at the goalie.

Crouching in goal, Vannie held up his hands and squinted as if he were about to suffer a great blow. He rocked on the balls of his feet and stared crookedly at shooters, swatting at the ball as if it were it an annoying wasp or fruitbat. He was so frail and gangly that when he tumbled to make a save, one feared that he would leave a strip of skin on the court. The net itself dwarfed him, and whenever he kicked the ball, he looked like a boy toeing the edge of a river, afraid to get his foot wet. During the warm-up, Vannie took a dozen easy shots, waved his hands, then shuffled over to the bench and began adjusting his shin pads, which fit him as did the rest of his kit: awkwardly.

If Team Canada was an odd collection of players, Vannie made them odder still. But while other teams might have reacted with disappointment and possibly anger at being burdened with a seemingly incapable goalie, the Canadians, instead, reminded themselves that they were lucky to have any goalie at all. At the end of their warm-up, Billy shouted, "C'mon over here, Vinnie, buddy," getting yet another player's name wrong. He slung an arm over his shoulder and said, "Grab the ball, Vinnie. Grab it whenever you can. Got it? You got it?" Down court, the Sierra Leoneans—who wore sky-blue jerseys and had entered the court dancing to "Walking on Sunshine" by Katrina and the Waves—gathered in a circle to secret their voices. One of the players' heads popped up, a hand covering his mouth to suppress his laughter.

The Sierra Leoneans—also known as the Mountain Lions—had been assembled largely by friends who'd played together in the streets of Freetown. At home, they lacked even the most basic tools of recreation, their equipment donated by NGOs. The Lions' trip to Melbourne had been financed by the HWC itself, and they were required to borrow balls from other teams to practise. The only courts in Freetown were street courts, and because most people live on a shaggy, if beautiful, hillside that slopes towards the sea, there were few plateaus to accommodate a proper field. While other countries—Ghana, Kenya, Brazil, and Argentina—had seen thousands of homeless people try out for their squads, the local sporting infrastructure in Sierra Leone was so poor that it was difficult to get the word out to potential players. Still, one of the Mountain Lions, a player named John, told me that excitement was building back home and that the team's scores were being posted in the main square, scribbled on great swaths of paper and tacked to one of Freetown's hand-painted billboards.

Because I'd travelled to Freetown a few years earlier, I introduced myself to the team before the beginning of the match. It didn't take long before we were trading the names of dance clubs with each other, shouting "Paddys!" and "Old School!" and yowling with delight. Inevitably, the talk turned to the war, or rather the post-war, and how the Leoneans were getting on in peacetime. Unlike the Zimbabweans, their bloody civil conflict was behind them and the notorious Liberian rebel marauder Charles Taylor was, at the moment, being tried for war crimes. And while Freetown was still largely a city without electricity, navigable roads, and any kind of new housing, a sense of hope pervaded a society that, only recently, had been savaged by sick, grinning rebels carrying machetes and guns.

John described his path to Australia; his father, a chief from the Fula tribe, had been a victim of the country's civil war, and his family was forced to flee once the rebels decided to exterminate them all one by one. "When war broke out," he said, "they put my brothers and sisters in a death camp. One day, they asked a few of us to forage for wood in the forest. My friend and I decided to run, leaving my siblings behind me. I just left. I walked for two weeks by myself. I ate wild fruit and yams, and because I was a scout, I knew a few things about the bush. When I escaped into Guinea, my friend and I taught Sierra Leone history to kids, free of charge, for nine months. After a while, we were told that it was safe to return to Freetown, but on January 6th, 1999, the rebels struck again. I had no means of escape. I can remember standing there and seeing two of my friends slaughtered in Terry Road. If you'd told me then that I'd be here in Melbourne, playing soccer, I would have branded you a madman."

While John was telling me his story, another player, Ollie, ambled up and raised his jersey, revealing a scar that ran from the bottom of his throat to his belly button. Like John, he'd crossed paths with the rebels, getting hit by gunfire and left to lie in the streets screaming. "People were imploring others to help me, but a rebel got to me first. He looked down at me, grinned, and slashed me with his machete. I thought I would die right there, but I was rescued and taken to the UN hospital, where they put me back together," he said. I echoed John's words about the absurdity of finding himself in Australia playing soccer, and he said, "This is something that no one could have ever imagined. When we told our friends we were coming here" he said, "people thought it was a joke, a prank. Not even my parents believed it was true."

Ollie couldn't say enough about what the event meant to him, but he did have a complaint: "The thing I enjoy least is the food," he moaned, shaking his head. "There is no rice or fish or guava. Only spaghetti and greens! This place is surrounded by water, but there is no fish. Why is that?" As it turned out, this was a common complaint among the Africans, but within days, organizers brought in bags of rice, cassava, and West African grains. A separate catering table was set up and the Leoneans' culinary yearnings were sated.

Despite the pasta—which I watched them savage nonetheless in the dining hall—Sierra Leone managed to control the opening minutes of their game versus Canada. It turned out to be a remarkable stroke of luck for Vannie that few of the Africans' shots found the net. This good fortune sparked the Canadians, who quickly surged into the lead, mostly because of Jerry's work in the offensive zone.

Not to devalue Jerry's shotmaking ability, but it's possible that the Leoneans had never played against anyone who moved as slowly as he did. Whenever he received a pass from Billy or Krystal, the first thing he did was trap the ball beneath his shoe like a man resting his foot on a curbside. The Mountain Lions danced around him waiting for his next move—so did P.J., for that matter—but Jerry maintained his stasis, waiting for his opponent's interest to wane before making a quick move that inevitably brought the ball closer to the net. In one instance, his ample belly and thick arms stilled before he pivoted and swung his leg, firing the ball into the far side of the goal. Dirty shots that clunked off defenders seemed beneath him, and, against Sierra Leone, his three goals found only the tight corners of the net or gaps in the goaltender's body that he'd failed to close.

While both Billy and Krystal's soccer skills were obvious, Jerry's were more subtle. Billy, for instance, wouldn't hesitate to try and smash the ball through the goaltender's sternum, while Krystal's quick feet and determination meant that she was forever trying to move the ball forward. Jerry's first move, however, was to control the ball to meet the demands of whatever form of attack he was, at that moment, diagramming in his head. His style was almost an affront to the West Africans' freewheeling soccer sensibilities, as predictable as it was effective. At the end of the first half, the score was 4–0 Canada, and you wouldn't have blamed the Lions if they'd thought these numbers had been conjured out of magic and deception. Even though the Africans were the livelier of the two teams, Jerry's efforts suspended reason and logic, giving his team the lead the way a magician produces a bouquet of flowers out of nothing.

The Sierra Leoneans—no strangers to black magic— steadied themselves during halftime and started the second half in better shape, putting two quick goals past Vannie, whose luck appeared to be giving out. But Krystal responded for Canada and Billy scored his first tournament goal, fattening their team's cushion. Still, the Leoneans pressed on, knowing that if they found the net, they would likely score. Then, with a handful of minutes left in the game—score 6–2, Canada—the West Africans were awarded a penalty kick after Vannie played the ball outside his half-moon crease.

As the ball was placed at centre court, Team Canada rained instructions on their fragile goalie. *Stand up, Vinnie! Put out your arms! Spread your legs! Keep your eye on the ball!* If Vannie heard any of this, you couldn't tell. He walked to the edge of his crease and stared straight ahead—half-grinning,

half-grimacing—his arms raised, gloves spidered open. Because street soccer penalties are more like hockey shoot-outs in that they allow the player to approach the goalie while dribbling, the African shooter nudged the ball forward and cruised towards Vannie. He cocked his leg and struck the ball hard—*whomp!*—his arms pistoning in the air. Vannie froze with the ball's flight, but the shot hit him in the legs, nearly driving him backwards into the net. The Canadians cheered as the African shooter grabbed his head in disbelief. When time expired, Vannie ran from the net into the arms of his new teammates, beads of sweat pinwheeling from his arms and face. Not only had Team Canada won their first game 7–5, but it looked like they'd made a friend, too.

After the game, Billy told Cristian: "It's not right to make the little guy stand in there for our next game against Ghana. They'll rip him up. They'll hurt him. Have you seen those guys shoot? C'mon, just let him have his moment." While Cristian weighed this advice, Billy added, "I mean, Christ, just look at him," gesturing to Vannie, who was sitting with Krystal along the riverbank. She had her arm around Vannie and kept telling him: "You played great, Vannie. You stole that game for us." Vannie's chest heaved with fatigue as he drained a series of water bottles.

"The guy just played the biggest game of his life," said Billy. "He's on a high right now. Let him enjoy it."

Cristian heeded Billy's advice. He approached Vannie and told him the team had decided to give Pommie the chance to tend goal for their next game. Krystal shot Cristian a look, but the coach ignored her as Vannie spoke for only the second time all day: "But I play. We win. Why I not play now?" Cris said that he was sorry, and the goalie shook his head regretfully. Billy came over and said, "You're a good goalie, man. Really good." Krystal added, "You're the best, Vannie. You'll be back. Don't worry, you'll see." Vannie listened, then ambled away, his look reflecting equal measures of pride and disgust.

9

OLE

SOFT

TITS

IF THE CANADIANS were feeling giddy after their win over the Mountain Lions, their hearts froze after getting their first look at Team Ghana. Every player was six feet tall, with long muscular arms and legs that rippled like the markings of a tide after a rainstorm. Wearing the stark black-and-white colours of their country's national team—the Black Stars—they lined up along their goal crease, where, on their coach's command, they quick-stepped side to side, knees hiked to their waists and hips swivelling. The players' shoulders torqued powerfully and their necks snapped back and forth in perfect rhythm while performing a syncopated warm-up to make Twyla Tharp envious. When the dance ended and the line broke, the players formed a circle and started punching a ball chest to chest, foot to foot, and head to head—*pomb! pomb! pomb!*—silent

save for equine huffs of breath and their highlife melody—
shalalaleylalalalaley!—which they hummed quietly as the ball
swept through the air. Downfield, the Canadians munched
on a bag of Starburst and looked worried.

Once the game started, the Ghanaians' performance was
no less smooth or assured. They were a dark ribbon of speed
on either side of the ball, a whorl of unforgiving selfishness.
They sailed five shots past Pommie before he snapped his
pointer finger at the knuckle while trying to stop one of the
Africans' whistling drives. The referee called time out and
waved for an attendant. With Vannie gone, the players were
forced to look to themselves to fill the goal. Cris wiped his
brow with his sleeve and called his team to the bench. Jerry
hid his head under his arm and Krystal bent over at the waist,
exhausted from the game's unrelenting pace. Billy, however,
had already moved towards the crease, where he gestured for
Pommie to lift his arms.

As a former pro, Billy had played through every kind
of injury. He'd suffered torn hamstrings, clipped tendons,
pinched nerves, bulging discs, strained biceps, bruised
kneecaps, strained flexors, shredded heels, squashed tes-
ticles, cleated buttocks, broken teeth, smashed cheekbones,
scorched lungs, traumatized kidneys, enraged bursa, gored
eye sockets, pretzelled fingers, and bloodied toes. The topog-
raphy of his body had been knifed, poked, and needled by a
ghoulish procession of doctors, and his skin was mapped
with a Spirograph of endless stitch marks.

Once, while playing for the North York Rockets, he'd
broken three metatarsal bones in his foot. Before the championship game he and his father had soaked his ankle cast
in a bucket of water and his father carved open the cast.

Billy gobbled a handful of pain killers given to him by the team doctor—OxyContins, the same drug that had nearly destroyed his life—and joined the team before their game, which they won. Later, he returned to his family doctor to have his foot reset, but the doctor handed him a pair of crutches and told him: "You're so fucking tough, use these."

Back when he was a professional footballer, pain and suffering were a kind of social currency. Billy and his teammates, especially the Europeans with whom he played in Austria and Switzerland, worked their battle scars as best they could. They preened themselves in hotel mirrors, and, spritzed with aftershave, stalked the discos of Bonn, Vienna, and Munich, the sleeve of their blazers not quite hiding an injured wing—*Oooh, does it hurt?*—their trouser legs savaged at the cuff to reveal an ankle or tibia or left foot crudely shrouded in plaster—*My baby, you are like a poor stricken bird.*

Once, Billy told me, "Let's face it: women love this shit. In Europe, I had a different beautiful woman every night. I had two girls, three, sometimes more. One time, I picked up a mother and a daughter. The mother wasn't so hot, but the daughter, man." He shook his head at the memory.

"I was 22, 23. Young, playing soccer, and getting paid. This wasn't Scarborough, man. This was *Europe*," he said, painting a scene of panties flung like silk scarves across a room, spumante bottles strewn across the carpet, an outline of coke rails dusted on a glass tabletop, and, over on the bed, a player and his evening's plaything lost under a mountain of rumpled bedsheets.

If no one else at the tournament had ascended farther in his career than Billy, you wouldn't have known it as he struggled to pull Pommie's yellow goalie's sweater over his head.

Because it was two sizes too small, it ballooned the saggy parts of Billy's upper body, making him look like an over-fed Teletubby. "Hey, Billy, nice tits!" yelled Cristian from the bench. He seemed grateful that the game's focus had been diverted from the fact that the Africans were pummelling his team. The Ghanaians, for their part, seemed not the slightest bit amused by the sight of an aging former pro rescuing his team from forfeit. Gathered at their bench, unglistening from the effortlessness of their play, they shook their legs in an attempt to stay loose during the game's time out. To them, Billy looked simply foolish, and as the referee tweeted the play alive, the Africans spared no time attacking the goal, trying to prove just how foolish he was.

The Ghanaians possessed none of the Lions' sunniness or just-happy-to-be-in-Melbourne spirit. At first, I found their competitiveness unbecoming, considering the nature of the event. But Chicken Baba told me later that most Africans were tired of going to international sporting events only to be humbled by better-trained, better-financed national teams. In street soccer, he said, it was possible to compete on a relatively even playing field, and this motivated the Africans to play as hard and well as possible, even if it meant running up the score.

"In the media, you hear a lot about how hard it is for Africans just to get to these kinds of events, but we are proud sportsmen," he said. "Still, unless it's maybe running or some other forms of track and field, we don't do very well against other countries, especially those from the West. But here, we can compete, and win, win, win. Millions of people play soccer in Africa, but only occasionally do our teams do well in the World Cup. You and I know the reasons for this, but that doesn't mean we have to be content with all of these disappointments. So, when Ghana thrashes Canada, it is not really personal," he said. "Well, it's maybe a little personal," he added, smiling.

Billy relished the opportunity to defend whatever Canadian pride the Africans had not already destroyed with their superior play. He rose to his opponents' advances, flinging his body at every screaming ball even though a towel-waving effort would have ensured a greater reserve of energy over the course of the tourney. But Billy wasn't built this way as an athlete or a person. Even though the Ghanaians paraded the ball up the court, and even though they buried at least a dozen more goals into the back of the net, there were few moments when Billy wasn't playing with his soul, hurtling across the crease and burying his shoulder into the turf to get to a ball. After scoring, the Ghanaians shouted in triumph, but in the aftermath of these celebrations, the sore-legged, soft-titted netminder rose to his feet and demanded more. In the end— and perhaps what galled the Africans most—no measure of scoring could dent the will of the Canadian goaltender. After he'd been beaten for the fifteenth time, he sprang to his feet, smiled, and pointed to the player who'd beaten him. The African goal scorer huffed and turned away insolently, as if, in fact, he hadn't beaten Billy at all.

$=10=$

WHERE THE FUCK IS DENMARK?

AFTER THE GAME, I met four middle-aged Danes vacationing in Australia. They'd come to cheer on Team Denmark and had enjoyed what they'd seen of the game.

"The Danes are very good, no?" they asked me.

"Yes, very good," I told them, though I hadn't seen them play.

"No one knows anything about Denmark," said one of the men. "But we are good at many things!"

"And not just sex!" chortled another.

"I'll have to take your word for it," I told them.

"Come to Denmark! You will see!"

"Maybe one day," I told them. "How are things going there, anyway?" I asked.

"Things are very good in Copenhagen. We have no big problems, not like elsewhere in the world," they said.

"How are things on the streets?" I asked.

"Oh, very good. We have social programs that help every-one. It is not an issue in Denmark."

"Don't you think it's strange, then, that there is a homeless team competing here? Things can't be that good if there's a street soccer program," I offered.

"Well, yes, there are people on the street. But they are lazy. And they want to live cheap. They are saving money!" one of them said.

"But the players who you just watched, who you cheered for…"

"Oh, they are a good team, yes. But, you know, anyone who's on the street is there because they want to be."

"You actually think people want to live in the metro and forage for food and suffer at the hands of police?"

"Well, not the beatings, no. But you saw the team, too. They are so happy out there. Trust me, my friend," he said, touching my arm. "Really, they like it this way."

Later, while leaving the field and walking to the tram, I told the team what the Danes had said. Krystal expressed the deepest outrage. "Denmark. What the fuck is Denmark any-way? People like that think they're superior, but they know nothing about the world. One thing about being homeless: you learn about people, you learn about yourself, you learn about the world," she said, growing angrier with each thought.

"Forget them, Krystal," said Billy. "They're not playing here. You are. What you've got—what we've got, as a team—they'll never know. I can't tell you how many times I've heard shit like that. Fucking hicks. Let them go back to fucking Denmark."

"Like, where the fuck is Denmark even?" she said.

"Exactly," said Billy, groaning as he climbed aboard the tram.

11

THE
SEARCH
FOR
STEVIE RAY

Drugs and booze are nice. When you're a
teenager, you smoke pot, have a giggle,
write a song, wander in the forest, watch the sunset, kill some
beers, go swimming, then pile back into your friend's car for
that long sleepy drive back into the city. The short films that
were screened in health class painted the evils of marijuana
and acid, showing the stoned gas station mechanic clipping
the brake wires of a sedan carrying a young family embark-
ing on their summer holiday. But after school, you'd go home,
fire up the stereo, and listen to Lou Reed's *Rock 'n' Roll Animal*,
Dylan's "Rainy Day Women #12 & 35," Little Feat's "China
White," The Stranglers' "Golden Brown," and "Chinese
Rocks" by Johnny Thunders. Then, at a party one night in
grade 11, someone passes you a joint. Just holding it makes
you feel like Jimi Hendrix.

In the summertime, my friends and I would go to a place called Balm Beach. We went there for two weeks every summer, the best summers of our teenage lives, whaling back lagers and ales and sucking smoke out of water pipes built from empty ginger ale bottles and tin foil. We called Balm Beach "Drunk Cottage," pretty much getting straight to the point. To us, partying was an Olympics of imbibing, a sport befitting the restlessness and stamina of our youth. We played the "Century Club," a drinking game in which 100 shot glasses of beer are downed in 100 minutes. The first time I did it, I reached 96, stood up, hurled, and continued the game. After the 100th shot, I fell over—we all fell over—four wobbly bodies pancaked against the grass, our dry tongues lolling across cheeks reddened by too much Ex, 50, Canadian, and Blue, the young Canadian alcoholic's four staples. Lying on our backs, we talked until the stars dimpled the sky and we finally gave out. Some gave out before others. Once, after my friend Joe fell asleep, we ran a trail of bread crumbs from the beach to his chest. He awoke wearing a vest of seagulls, pecking him from head to toe.

My friend Eddie was our ringleader. He was tall and skinny, quick brained, and cunning. Once, we got arrested for smoking hash in Eddie's parent's Pacer, the old AMC bubble car that looked like a goiter on wheels. When the police searched us in a nearby field, they checked the front band of Eddie's underwear. Eddie told the cop: "That's all me down there, sir."

Eddie was a master with the morning's pipe. He'd recline on the couch in his pyjamas lighting the bong as the sun streamed through the dirty square windows of the drafty cottage, calling our names, one by one, to take the day's first hit.

Within minutes, we'd be on the floor in stomach-cramping laughter. Somebody put his elbow through the window. A coffee pot caught fire. We howled until empty of laughter, then drifted off to our wood-panelled rooms, crawling under bedspreads, trying to sleep off the deep-motoring buzz.

When you're a teenager, you go until you can go no more. And even then, you go. You shake off the hangover bruises, dried puke, and silent, worried stares of your parents and family. You smoke and drink every day. You're 16. You've never had more fun in you're entire life, and you might not ever again.

But for every kid who gets high and writes poetry and hears OK Computer like they've never heard it before, there are those who are destroyed by drugs. While my friends and I smoked weed on cottage porches and summertime beaches, people like Krystal got high in desolation, in empty sheds and garages. Sometimes, she'd find herself riding in a strange car going nowhere, drawn to others who shared her need, their faces lost in blue smoke. Billy partied, too, with young men at soccer camp, looking for a release, team bonding, no big deal. Then he discovered painkillers and then cocaine, escalating his high to reach whatever buzz the pot and hash couldn't deliver. The night he was arrested, he'd started arguing with his girlfriend. Within an instant, he'd become a volcano of rage, tearing pictures off the wall, shattering glass, smashing the coffee table, hurling the television across the room, savaging the mattress, breaking plates, and making cyclopian holes in the drywall with his fists. The cops struggled to push him into their cruiser. They threw him in jail, where he lingered in the aftermath of his rage. When I asked him if this episode was the first step towards getting clean, he said,

"You're never really clean, even if you're not using. You've lived through these things—the highs and the lows—and you're never the same afterwards. The truth is, if you put a line of coke in front of me, I'd probably do it. I have to put myself in the position where that sort of thing won't happen again."

Although one of the lessons of the HWC is that the causes of homelessness are many, it wasn't hard to notice that a lot of the players' lives had nearly been destroyed by drug abuse. At times, my experience here was like walking into a novel written by Hubert Selby Jr. or Irvine Welsh. I met no fewer than twenty players who'd been out of jail for less than a year. One Swedish player told me that, "It started with a beer. Then a joint. Then a needle. Next thing I knew, I'd lost my house and my car. It happens fast, man. I tried to quit for seven years, in and out of treatment, until I'd finally had enough. Everyone else on this team has been through the same thing. Two of us are from Stockholm, the other two are from Goethenburg, but we've met the same people on the streets. For our team in Australia, it's not about winning or losing games. Just staying sober is our victory."

Almost the entire Czech team was made up of recovering drug addicts. Their manager, a soft-voiced, long-haired fellow named Marcel, told me that while their homeless soccer program wasn't necessarily centred on recovering addicts, they could have sent multiple teams of players who'd been addicted to Pervitin, a Czech-made methamphetamine that was the scourge of many young Eastern Europeans. "There have always been drug and alcohol problems in Czechoslovakia and now the Czech Republic, both before and after the revolution. In Communist times, if you lived on the street, the government would throw you in jail. Unless you could prove that you had a home, you disappeared and were sometimes never heard from again. If you were an alcoholic, there was no support system. And while things are better now, there's still a stigma attached to people who have a problem. And with Pervitin, it's a whole new issue. Lots of young people are dying or living hard on the streets."

Marcel was reluctant to boast about his own players' triumphs over addiction, aware, as many counsellors are, of chronic recidivism and the lifelong process of recovery. Still, he offered one story about the fortunes of his team's captain, who had lived on and off the streets for eight years. "When he came to us," said Marcel, "he was 80 pounds and had the look of a very sad ghost. But we helped him get through the rehabilitation process, got him a bed in the shelter, and found him work at a local Starbucks. His employers knew nothing about his past until, one day, he was interviewed on Czech television prior to leaving for Melbourne. He told his whole story, and when he returned to work, the people at Starbucks were in tears. He'd been terrified about revealing what he'd gone through, but his co-workers supported him and even gave him more responsibility in the café. Stories like this give me hope for greater society. They're cheering us back at the shop, and every day he calls there and gives them the results."

There were two American players who, like me, grew up loving music and sports. They'd gotten stoned in high school, goofed around, gone to shows. One of them was the team's first-string goaltender, Tim, a Chicagoan who lived in North Carolina. Tim was a great tank of a man, with cropped silver hair and arms the size of throw pillows. One of the first things he'd done in Melbourne was reach into his pocket to help one of the Liberian women, who'd removed herself from a game after not having money to buy sanitary products. I told him that because the Americans had colonized Liberia, its flag was a near duplicate of the Stars and Stripes and that young Liberians pledge allegiance every morning in school.

"I didn't know that," he said, his gaze falling to the ground.

Tim and I were the same age: 45. We'd both been raised in a privileged suburban cocoon. He'd gone to private school and was brought up in what he said was a very loving Christian family. His parents had enrolled him in soccer, and he learned to love all sports, dreaming of one day becoming a pro athlete himself. His favourite goaltender was one-time Chicago Blackhawk Eddie Belfour, who, while being an all-star goalie, is also noted for allegedly offering the police a billion dollars to let him out of their squad car, right before he vomited on himself.

But after years of partying and smoking dope, Tim turned to hard drugs and eventually got caught in the web of crack addiction. "I was living in a crack house for quite a while," he said, lighting a smoke. "And while I am and always was a very friendly, loving person, I did everything I had to do to survive. It got very ugly, very bad. It used to be that I'd give you the shirt off my back, but while I was high, it didn't matter. You become very mean and selfish. It's all about that next hit, and you'll do anything you have to do to get it." When I asked Tim if he could remember the turning point in his life, he said that "it happened in the crack house, when I was almost hit from behind in the head with a hammer. I had some money in my pocket, and the others knew it. The only thing that saved me was seeing the assailant's shadow on the wall. If I hadn't seen him seconds before he was about to attack me, I'd be dead. Funny thing is, it was only a few weeks before coming here that I saw this same person at one of our soccer team's practices in Charlotte. Personally, I have nothing against him. He's trying to get his shit together and that's good. He tried to kill me, but it was all just part of the scene. It's a part of my life that I'm done with, but I hope he makes it, too."

Another American player was a Texas-born crystal-meth addict named Tad, who had the look of a deep-eyed hound still hopeful after years of scavenging the rain-swept streets. Before the tournament started, some managers suggested that the Americans would try to build a competitive roster rather than draft players who might benefit from the experience, having been disappointed with how the team placed in previous years. But this supposition was unfounded. Not only did Team USA struggle to win as the Canadians had, but players like Tad possessed very little chalkboard knowledge or innate sense of the game. Unlike Tim or Billy, he'd played hardly any soccer before joining the homeless program in Austin, but, to me, he emerged as the tournament's star, a player who'd come to Melbourne determined to meet as many people as possible and who absorbed every succulent detail that comes with travelling to a new place far from home.

"Many years ago, I was married and living in New Orleans," said Tad. "After my divorce, I started working for the mob, the NOM, we called it. My wife's brother was married to a girl named Corrina; she had a high, squeaky voice and managed a strip club called Action Central, the biggest in New Orleans. My first job was to take care of her. I was given information—the information proved to be false, but it was classified—and I was put in certain positions where I was asked to share it. I didn't, and I earned my stripes. After that, the bosses handed me a buttload of methamphetamines—I had to hold them for hours—and when they came back, they asked me if I'd used any of it. I said I hadn't, and they said, 'Not any? Not even a bit?' I told them, 'No, man, it's not mine.' And that was it. I was in.

"Basically, I became a dope whore, a male version of a moll. I took care of all of the women who were high up. It was important that I was around because, in certain instances, it's essential that a man and a woman be seen together. It makes everything seem kind of normal, so that when the feds, the cops, whomever, ask what you're doing, you can say, 'We're having dinner, we're making babies.' I did this for a while until, one day, I woke up and I was the man. THE MAN. I was doing deals from Dallas and Fort Worth, driving the finest cars, the fastest Mustangs. I had the best-looking strippers and the best dope. It might seem whacked in a sense, but I felt like I was making it, climbing up the ladder with all of this approval. I felt good, and I was good at my job, but like anything, I got tired of it. The world of dope was a fallacy. I wanted a real woman, and I wanted my life back. I was somebody important, but I wanted something real. When you fall in with the wrong crowd, you sort of lose track of that; you forget that a fulfilling and normal life is possible. I've done things that I regret that I never wanna talk about, but the bad things I did I usually did to bad people. It's how I justify them. There's not one junkie or addict or drunk who's not worth fixing, but someone who's running around ripping people off, shooting them, raping helpless women, that's not right, either. There were people I knew who'd blow your kneecaps off and rape your old lady just to get your drugs or your money. Those people have to be dealt with, and that became part of my job, too. It wasn't what I'd bargained for, but, in the end, it's what all junkies end up doing.

"I got sent to prison. I was locked up for ten months for the unauthorized use of a vehicle. They put me in a room and asked me questions to which they knew the answers. When I wouldn't address them, they'd shove my food through the hole and spill it. I was tasered, pepper-sprayed. It wasn't about not telling on someone; it was just that they were just as bad and mean and disrespectful on the inside as they were on the outside. The guards couldn't handle my attitude, either. They'd say to me, 'You know you're going to lockdown, right?' I'd say, 'Wait a minute. I'm supposed to be upset about this? You want me to go into this cell, and you're gonna bring me my food? Hey, I'm down with this!' I met a lot of great people who helped me turn my life around in jail. I graduated high school there, got my diploma. If I'd been in a little longer, I might have got my university degree, too.

"When I got out, I started using again, and I ended up in Colorado Springs weighing 85 pounds. I was cooking dope, slinging it. I graduated from cosmetology school, but I never went through with my state board approval. I went to deejay school, but they said I didn't have the voice for it. I was strung out all the time and had all of my teeth pulled.

"Then one night, I was waiting for my connection in East Texas to call and it hit me like a ton of bricks. I wasn't crying, but my eyes were watering. It felt like a release. My girlfriend said, 'Baby what's wrong? Why are you crying?' She got paranoid and I told her, 'I've had enough. I'm not scoring, I'm not re-upping. She looked at me and said, 'C'mon baby, get back in the game.' When I told her, 'No,' she looked at me and said, 'You motherfucker.' A few days later, I called her house and someone else answered. I could hear my girlfriend in the background ordering whomever was there to go to where I was staying and kill me. It didn't stop me from loving her and, truth be told, it actually made me kind of horny. But that day, I walked away. I was walking down the highway, headed back to Louisiana. I was alone on the road in flip flops and shorts and it was raining. I asked myself, 'Why am I walking back there?' I immediately turned around and I had an awesome feeling. I was so happy that I wasn't going back to the place where all of this had started in the first place. I ended up on the streets of Dallas and from there, I headed to Austin. I've been there ever since. One of my first nights on the streets, I turned a corner and found myself standing in front of a statue of Stevie Ray Vaughan, who was born in South Oak Cliff. I was also born in South Oak Cliff. There it was. The circle had closed. I was finally a free man."

— 12 —

L'ALTRI

AZZURRI

As with every international soccer tournament the world over—including home-
less ones—the Italians were represented in Melbourne,
too. But none of the players possessed the gleaming perfect
teeth and silken hair that define Italy's traditional football
heroes. They were L'Altri Azzuri—"the other blue," referring
to the national team's uniforms—largely made up of African-
Italians and other immigrants new to the country. If that
weren't enough, the team's coach was a Pole named Bogdan
Kwappik, a contemplative fellow who'd chosen his players
based on an incident that had occurred the previous winter,
when a young African man had been beaten to death by thugs
in the streets of Milan. Considering Italy's often xenopho-
bic sporting climate—over the years, black athletes have
been taunted with bananas—it was a bold gesture to select
a foreigner as a coach, to say nothing of fielding a lineup of

players—*clandenistas*, Bogdan called them—who were born elsewhere.

Before coaching the homeless team, Bogdan worked with people from multicultural backgrounds who'd fallen on hard times. One night at the tournament's dining hall—where, like the Africans, the Italians found the pasta wanting—he told me: "I became involved with the program as a way to help those I knew, and from this, my eyes were opened to a much greater community of suffering. At first, people raised an eyebrow that the job had been given to a Pole, and I still get criticized because of who I am. A lot of people still have something against immigrants—not just in Italy, but everywhere—and we have a lot of problems with sponsorship. Some people think that this is not an Italian team. While there's a certain pride in the team after we win, it doesn't last for very long."

The coach had scoured Milanese shelters looking for men and women willing to join the program. One of these players, a young Colombian named Claudia, had been bullied by gangs as a poor teenager in her homeland until she was forced to mule heroin by freighter to Italy, where she was apprehended and sent to prison. There, she told me, she "learned to sew and gain other skills, and, in a lot of ways, it was an improvement over life in Colombia. But I was without my freedom, and after being released, I had no idea how I would survive in this new country. The team helped me find a job, shelter, and gave me a new set of friends. And Bogdan, Bogdan encourages me to do things I never dreamed of doing."

Another member of L'Altri Azzuri was a six-foot-five African named Theodore from Côte d'Ivoire whose family had been murdered, en masse, by roving death squads, partly because they were wealthy, and partly because his father was a respected local politician. Theodore was the only member of his family who escaped, moving by way of Ghana into Italy. He was granted asylum but ended up on the streets. By selecting him and Claudia, the Italian team operated contrarily to any other national team that Italy had previously sent abroad.

Bogdan had guided Italy to victory in the 2005 HWC in Scotland, an achievement that was all the more impressive considering that two Italians players were refused entry into the country, forcing the coach to play with a ragtag collection of substitutes provided by the host country. After returning from the tournament, he was discouraged to discover that no one in the Italian media wanted to talk about their victory. To many, the championship was poxied, having been won with and against players too lazy or reprobate to play any kind of real soccer. As a result, Bogdan went on a five-day hunger strike. His efforts made the news, but for largely the wrong reasons. The coach was *pazzo*, as unhinged as the rest of his players.

A few months after his hunger strike, Bogdan lost his job. He had great difficulty finding another one. Soon, he was forced out of his apartment and sought refuge on the streets of Milan. He lived in his car, parking it in empty alleyways, abandoned fields, and city construction sites, the HWC trophy tipped on its side on the floor of the backseat, its dull silver finish reminding him of his former achievement. When Italy's homeless team's manager, a smooth-voiced, young Italian architect named Allesandro, first met Bogdan, he discovered that the coach had spent countless nights at one of his firm's building sites. When he told me this, he tented his fingers over his eyes, hiding the tears that had gathered at the memory.

Despite being homeless himself, Bogdan continued to run the program. He looked for work by day, then ran practice at night. Clearly, if you couldn't play for him, you couldn't play for anyone.

Things had gone well for the Italians through the beginning of the tournament. But it wasn't long before their fortunes soon went south. News reached the other teams that someone from the team's management—either Bogdan or Allesandro; no one was saying—had made an error in assembling their roster, naming two players to the team who'd competed in previous tournaments. This was a serious red flag for HWC organizers, as well as for other teams. After being called on their indiscretion, Allesandro and Bogdan began canvassing others for support. This further rankled the HWC potentates, who felt that the Italians were manipulating tournament members instead of relying on the organizers to pass final judgement. It didn't help that they were earmarked to host the next HWC, in Milan. At one point, Allesandro pleaded his case to me, even though I was the farthest thing from a voting delegate. "We have made a severe error," he told me, "and we stand by this. We are not saying that we did not do wrong, but we are still hoping that these players can play, because they have worked very hard. It is our fault, the management's," he said. "If anyone should be punished, it is us. They shouldn't punish the players."

It all sounded reasonable to me, but the other team's managers were not as forgiving. There was a heated council meeting one morning, which saw the Russian coach storm out in protest. After further discussion, it was decided that the Italians would have to play the rest of the tournament without these players lest they jeopardize their standing as the host of next year's tournament. After the decision, Bogdan told the organizers: "If we win, we want to win honestly." I asked Paul what he thought of the whole business, and he said, "This is what this tournament is becoming. People make mistakes. Certainly, Bogdan has given enough of himself to homelessness in Italy that he should be allowed this error. But some managers don't think it was a mistake. They think the Italians did it on purpose. That we're even having this discussion sort of shows you what direction the HWC is headed."

The day after the organizers' decision, I found Allesandro strolling the riverside boulevard by himself. I told him that Canada didn't support the decision, that it thought the players should play. "Ahhh," he said, sighing. "I am trying. We all are trying. Maybe we try too hard and, as a result, these things happen. But the players," he said, rubbing his face. "The players are very disappointed and I feel like shit for them."

Then he started crying. "I feel the worst for Bogdan," he said, sobbing. "After all he's been through. Now, this," he said, reaching for a tissue in his bag. I told him not to worry too much about the coach. It only stood to reason that after all he'd been through, Bogdan would be okay.

"In Polish," he told me, breaking down a second time, "the name 'Bogdan' means victory. *Victory*," he said, dragging out the last syllable while tightening his hands into fists. "He is a great man, and now, he must go through this," he said. Allesandro couldn't bear the fact that he'd created a measure of sadness among a group of players whose lives had seen enough misery, pain, and disappointment. L'Altri Azzuri ended up bowing out of the tournament early and their outlawed players watched from the stands, but, for Allesandro and Bogdan, the event had become about something more than just winning or losing or working to raise the profile of the world's homeless. It was about not letting each other down, even after you did.

=== 13 ===

THE

RUSSIANS

CANADA'S NEXT GAME yielded an opponent even more formidable than the Ghanaians: Team Russia. Even though they lacked a traditional soccer rivalry, Canada versus Russia evoked an emotional reaction because of the events of September 1972, when a heavily favoured hockey team made up of NHL stars from Canada challenged the Russian national team to an eight-game series played over four weeks in both countries. It was the first time a collection of pro athletes had competed behind the Iron Curtain, and the series was decided in the last 34 seconds of game eight in Moscow when Paul Henderson, who was not very highly regarded, scored the winning goal and became an instant national hero. As it turned out, the events of Canada's fourth game of the 2008 HWC would be less fraught with national intrigue, but the team's hero would be just as unlikely.

Team Russia was a heavy presence in Melbourne. The coach, Arkady Tyurin—the one who had refused to vote on the Italian issue—ran the homeless program in St. Petersburg and was the editor-in-chief of the local homeless newspaper. His team's slogan—SHUT UP AND PLAY—reflected his seriousness about the game and the fact that his team had closed ranks against the rest of the competing nations. Nonetheless, having spent a lot of time in his native country, I badly wanted to interview him. Since I'd been through this scenario before with the often impregnable hockey community in Russia, I knew that constant badgering would be required to gain his consent, even though I was careful not to get in the way of his team's preparations. Still, because of my fondness for Bogdan, and because of Arkady's lack of support for him, I felt compelled to corner him.

During my visits to Moscow, I'd met lots of hockey players who'd fallen on hard times, post-Communism. They lived in small apartments with very little income after years of being treated as royalty in the former Soviet Union. In some cases, they'd turned to alcohol to deal with their reduced circumstances. In a country where nearly everything had been provided by the state, many former athletes had been forgotten and some lived on a pittance earned while barnstorming a wintertime legends' hockey circuit played in cold rinks in remote outposts.

When I finally found Arkady sitting by himself along the riverside embankment, the first thing I did was share my experiences among the hockey old-timers. I told him how I'd accompanied the Russian National Old-timers team—many of whose players had competed in the 1972 series—to the industrial city of Barnaul. There, I was given a national team sweater to match my equipment, but languished on the bench for the entire first period. Then the coach, Bichokov, sent me out for a few shifts in the second period, and by the third, I was taking a regular shift. It ranks among the greatest sporting memories of my life, and I told this to Arkady.

After finishing my story, I realized that I had been doing all the talking and hadn't asked him a single question. A moment of silence passed between us. He sniffed and looked around gravely, and as I steeled myself for his upbraiding, he pointed to his head. "You see my hair?" he said, somewhat cryptically. "I wear it this way because of Guy Lafleur."

We embarked on the kind of rambling, ravenous hockey talk that only a Canadian and a Russian could produce. It turned out that Arkady had played hockey for Spartak of Novosibirsk, and he could name the Russian club teams of all of the players I'd met in Moscow. He'd travelled to Montreal in 2006 as part of an international street newspaper editor's conference, and, remembering the event, he said, "My life can be divided into two parts: before the New Year's Eve Red Army game in 1975 versus Montreal, and after." When I returned to Toronto weeks later, I found a photo in my inbox of Arkady kneeling in front of a painting of the Montreal Canadiens' crest.

Arkady had had a happy childhood living in a town 30 kilometres east of Novosibirsk in Siberia, a city that had been erected solely for the purpose of scientific research. His mother was a doctor and his father an engineer, and his town was as free a place as could have existed in the former Soviet Union. "The best minds in Russia lived there, and you were allowed to freely express your political views," he said. "I learned to speak different languages, and the exchange of information between other countries was common, in the interests of scientific development."

When he was 15 years old, Arkady and his friends spray painted ALL OF THE OLD KREMLIN GUYS, GET OUT on the wall of his school. It was a rebellious gesture born from the freedom of expression allowed in his community, but it did not sit well with the authorities. His actions precipitated a visit by the KGB, the first in a series during his teenage years. Eventually, Arkady grew disillusioned by the community's double standard and fled Siberia for St. Petersburg, where, he said, "I thought I would go and die. To be killed. My life was over. It was finished. I felt like it was at the end."

He survived on the streets for eleven years. He picked up work wherever he could: cleaning waste in a shipbuilding plant, where he was paid in crude spirits sweetened with mouldy raspberries; unloading vegetables for an Azerbaijani pedophile; providing nighttime guard duty for offices; and cleaning homes for a handful of coins. Still, none of these jobs provided enough of an income for him to afford proper lodging. "Being a young man," he told me, "I thought that I was an important role model in the anti-Soviet resistance, but now my soul is a lot lighter. The KGB doesn't define my life anymore, because if you let them define you, you play into their hands. Still, if the Soviet Union doesn't exists in terms of government, it continues to exist as a mindset. Only now, as an adult, I realize that there are other ways to fight this problem."

At the end of our discussion, Arkady handed me a book. It was small enough to fit in the palm of my hand and was called *The Homeless Book of Life*. It was published, he told me, to illuminate homelessness in the former Soviet Union and to serve as a kind of handbook for those who found themselves living on the streets. Arkady's contribution was a list of suggestions for those living without food, decent work, or proper shelter and contained items such as:

> › Rats can fall from the ceiling
> › Using a cigarette filter can make a razor to cut boxes
> › Even a small piece of cheese will prevent your teeth from rotting
> › No matter how funny your clothes look, wear them as long as they are warm and clean
> › Don't steal from where you are working, even if the employer is cheating you
> › The word 'pedophile' sounds like 'getveran' in Azerbaijani
> › You can do without shaving provided you clean your teeth twice a day
> › Don't use gasoline on wounds
> › When your shoes are clean, it's easier to smile
> › If you really want to, you can get out of the basement

Lawyers, doctors, and street musicians had also contributed to the book. In one chapter, musician Mikhail Sidorov compared his efforts travelling to the south of Russia to that of Dustin Hoffman's character in Midnight Cowboy, writing about how the north is full of "snow, rats, and criminals," while the south is a land of "grapes, mandarins, warmth, and palm trees in the sand." Addressing the uncertainty of homeless life in the former Soviet Union, he described how he was once harboured by a religious order St. Elizabeth the New Martyr, who "turned orthodox on the spur of the moment...

dragging the vagrant by his legs into [a] cage while clinging to the bars. [There was] no sleep for anybody. If the vagrant is lucky, they will put him near the radiator, or perhaps leave him as he fell. And in the morning, if he is still alive, they will kick him out on his backside shouting: 'Go away, dear, and may the Lord be with you!'"

I thanked Arkady for the book, but before we parted ways, I warned him: "Tomorrow. The Canadians. Don't forget what happened in 1972." He laughed for the first time, and said: "What happened in Game One or in Game Eight?"

"Let's just ice the turf," I said. "And play it all over again."

Having already won a HWC title, the Russians were heavily favoured in Melbourne. Many agreed that Canada would have to play a remarkable game to acquit themselves without embarrassment. Billy and Jerry approached the game with a veteran's nonchalance, while Krystal fidgeted nervously before the match, which would take place in the main stadium at Federation Square, an appropriate setting considering the two teams' sporting symbiosis. Of all of the players, Krystal seemed prone to carrying the fortunes of her life in her expressions, her attitude, and the occasionally sloping mien of her shoulders. I thought about what Krystal had told me the previous day, and how what she'd said might have weighed on her thoughts as Team Canada began warming up for the important game.

"You try and put certain things out of your head, but our decisions stay with us; some of them are wrong, some of them right," she'd said. "Whenever I make wrong decisions—stealing, smoking weed, coming home late—I feel like my mom. My bad decisions started when I was 15. There was a lot of fighting between my adopted father and me because he was very strict. He expected a lot from me, especially with sports. He pushed me very hard, and I got angry, but I kept it bottled up. I snuck out of the house, hung around with bad kids I'd met in high school, started smoking weed, failed grade nine. My parents sent me to a private school—St. Jude's in Kitchener—which was worse, even though I got all of my credits. I was the only black kid, and everyone called me names. The school had a small cafeteria, and it was hellish. At lunch, I was bombarded by taunts and name-calling. I'd take my books, find a classroom, and do my work. That's when I started writing poetry, which helped me get through it all.

"My parents brought me back to the same school where I'd got into trouble, and, of course, I fell back into the same shit. That's when I ran away for good. My friends had a car and all of my clothes were in bags. There was a house where I could stay, but I was kicked out pretty soon after I moved in. The friends who helped me run away weren't my friends, after all. I ended up finding another room in another house, full of crazy people. The guy who owned it was a dirty man, bringing home young girls, and I didn't feel safe. I was sexually abused and it was very bad. One night, I was drunk and not stable and I went into a Tim Hortons, came around to the counter, and stole whatever money I could get my hands on. The guy who owned the house where I was living found out and threw me into the streets with all of my stuff. It was seven in the morning. I had nowhere to go. I lived in garages, broke into sheds. Sometimes, I slept in friends' closets so that their parents wouldn't find out. Sometimes, people would offer their place, but when I showed up, the door would be locked and so I just stayed up. I was drunk and stoned a lot of the time; I had nothing. I hardly ever went to school. Then my natural brother, Jason, found me and asked if I wanted to come live with him in Toronto. To some people, it might not seem like much, but it was home. My home."

I asked her if she'd thought a lot about home while in Melbourne, but, after considering her reply, she waved her hand in front of her face and asked, "Hey, are you going to bring Eric's gloves to the game?" Lifting whatever gravity had fallen upon our conversation, I told her that, yeah, I would, and before the start of the game, she instructed me to "slap them right here, on the crest, for good luck." I did so, then slapped the rest of the team. (Billy shrieked: "Get away with those things!" But he soon consented after a quick chase around the court.) Eventually, the referee—a grave-looking African fellow with a shaved head and yellow shoes—tweeted his whistle and called the players to mid-court. Krystal ran to the half-line, buoyant and alive in the realm of the field.

As they had before every other game, the Canadians had to look over their shoulders to remind themselves who was in goal. This time, it was a fellow named Ned, another Aussie reserve. Like Dove, Ned had the appearance of someone who was far older than the date on his birth certificate would suggest. He was 40, but looked 55 after years in and out of juvenile detention and prison and a prolonged stay on the streets. He was a self-confessed junkie who was trying to get straight. His coach, George Halkias, told me that "there are huge drug and anger issues with Ned. He's been trying to deal with it in the year and a bit that I've known him, and he's had his ups and downs. But at least he's trying. He's gonna have good days and bad days. All you can do as coach is try and motivate him. The rest is up to him."

Ned grew up in Sydney. As a kid, he bounced from mother to father, both of whom were alcoholics working in pubs. "The only good thing my mother ever did for me," he said, "was put me in soccer, which was pretty much a way of keeping me out of her hair. Back then, I did whatever I wanted to do. I moved out and started living on the streets when I was 14. I couldn't live with my father, who was a hot-headed bloke. I had a rough 10 years. I'm clinically depressed and I delved into drugs, alcohol, gambling. I didn't give two shits about people. I was by myself. I depended on myself. I grew up by myself. I taught myself street rules. I was self-managed, and when I left school, I couldn't read. I taught myself how to read, starting with kids' books. Now I'm reading novels, not big ones, but at least I'm reading. My math isn't good, but I'm a concreter by trade, and you don't really need math in concrete, unless you're the boss. It's pretty decent money. I've learned to survive on a lot less.

"On the streets, you learn where to sleep, how to be safe, who to trust, who to mingle with. You learn not to mingle with the wrong people. Fall in with the wrong crowd and the next thing you know you're standing at Kings Cross in Sydney with a weapon in your pants, dealing drugs, trying to make money. After a while, it becomes your way of making a living. You think it's normal, even though it's not. I ended up doing two and a half years in jail. I'm not proud of it, but now I can tell people I meet on the street that that's how they're gonna end up. It's inevitable. I still live in a bad situation—I've got a place in Flemington in the north part of the city—and there are drugs everywhere, Sudanese warfare, lots of fights. I just want get out of it, but it's not easy. In Australia, it's hard to get private housing. Rent has gone up, bills have gone up.

Water bills are huge because there's no water in the country. In the past year, I've met people on the street who used to be rich, pulling $90,000 a year doing computer support. Their wives left them and they've been thrown into the hot fire. Sometimes, they come to me and question me because I'm the one who has experience. I'm a veteran of the streets at 40 years old.

"Don't get me wrong, I'm grateful to live in this country. We've got a guy who played with us last year, his name is Manning. He used to work in the diamond mines in Sierra Leone, which is basically a death sentence for whoever goes down there. Another one of our players is named Lorenso. He came to Australia in a crate. He lived in it for two months. His toilet was a bucket in the corner. He spent two years in a detention centre in Iran. He was classified as a communist in his country, and they were going to kill him, so he escaped. You hear these kinds of stories and realize that, really, you've got no excuse. We live in a beautiful country with beautiful beaches, beautiful women. I can buy a five-dollar ticket and be in the purest, most beautiful part of the world. I know that there's a way out of this shit. It's hard, but it's there if I want it."

Ned hoped that he could use the tournament to get straight. It was a formula that had worked, at least partly, for others. Ned wanted to be like Eric, who had stayed straight three nights a week with the team in Toronto, nearly halving his weekly habit. He bargained that the crackling endorphins of sport would fill whatever hole the heroin helped fill, and, at times, a hopefulness forced its way into his eyes, like sunlight seeping through a broken doorframe. When I suggested to Billy that Ned was a good addition to the team, he reacted as the Aussie coach had: with suspicion. He told me that Ned had boasted to him about how, just a few nights earlier, his 17-year-old girlfriend had attacked a policeman with a baseball bat. Ned told Billy that he was proud of what she'd done, because, in his words, "nobody hates cops more than me. She's a good kid. I'll keep her."

Still, Ned possessed a certain gritty self-determination that provided Team Canada with something they'd lacked in previous games. His tight-jawed resilience instilled in the players the sense that coming to Melbourne wasn't only about seeing the world and playing a little footie but also about winning. The first thing he'd done after being delivered to Paul was to ask for a Team Canada baseball hat and sweater— "I'm one of youse now," he'd said, giving his teammates pause—and seeing him dressed in red and white as he patrolled the net with a nail-eating fervour goosed the team's effort, for they came out kicking and swinging as soon as the game began.

The lead changed hands every few minutes. The action travelled back and forth up the court—Billy booting a shot from mid-court under the crossbar into the goal; the Russians—young, white, fit, technical, and exact—scoring in the time it took me to draw a breath; and Jerry playing hide and seek with the ball in the corner, ordering a corndog from the concessionaire, then licking his finger and holding it out to test the breeze before back-heeling a shot through the goaltender's wickets. All of this was played out to Ned's dull roar from the goal crease, imploring his team to "Go get 'em boys! Go get 'em good!" By halftime, it was 4–3 Russia, but it was still either team's game to win. Just as the Russian hockey team in '72 had relaxed against Canada heading back to Moscow with a two-game lead, so had the Russian footballers measured their opponent too lightly. I watched them huddle at their bench, where perhaps they reminded each other that even though their side had destroyed every other opponent so far in the tournament, the Canadians maybe remembered '72 a little more clearly, not forgetting that their hockey players had won with their backs against the wall, too.

As a result, the Russians struck quickly and fastidiously. Soon, it was 6–3, Russia, but Billy answered with a fluke goal that boinged off a forest of legs. The Canadians kept pressing until one of the Russian defenders ran at Krystal hard, shouldering her off the ball as she dribbled it up court. When this happened, I recalled what a friend of mine—a Muscovite, Yulia Ochetova—had once told me: that, traditionally, people of colour have suffered great discrimination throughout Russian history. "Russia is no better than anywhere else. It is a racist country," she said, especially after meeting travellers romanced by their visit to the former Soviet Union. Whether the Russian had gone hard into Krystal because of her race was uncertain, but whatever the context, the Russian footballers' tackle had caused an infraction, and the tenor of the game, and its momentum, rested on the feet of the young girl from Regent Park, who steadied her gaze as she strolled to mid-court to take her first penalty kick.

Back in Toronto, Krystal had told me: "Even when things were bad in life, soccer was never far from my mind. My mom was a really good track athlete, and my brother and grandmother say that it's one of the reasons I'm good at soccer, too. When I was living on the streets, I tried to get back into the game, but it was very hard. I didn't have money to pay for jerseys or transportation to and from the field. When I got to Toronto and to my brother's place, I'd take the soccer ball and kick it around in the park with the kids. Then, one day, this fellow, whose name was Monte, came by and asked if I wanted to play for the homeless team at Moss Park at Queen and Sherbourne, so I did. Before I came to Australia, I made a countdown calendar at home. In life, you can do things the easy way or the hard way. It's weird. Sometimes, you have to know what's wrong to know what's right."

Before Krystal took her shot, she tapped her crest twice— once for her late mother, and again for her grandmother— and kissed her hand while peering into the sky. The stands were filled to near capacity, with hundreds more fans watching from the piazza, their voices muted in anticipation. Krystal flicked the ball forward, then moved in on the Russian keeper.

She took three steps, then shot. The goalie leapt into the air and flung his arms up, but the ball screamed into the high corner of the net. Krystal collapsed to the ground, her fists balled at her sides. Ned roared ecstatically and clapped his gloves, while the rest of the team rushed to her. Krystal rose from the floor and wagged a finger at the crowd, defiant after her score.

After the game, she told me, "I was thinking of so many things before taking that shot: all of the people I've known, my family, my nephews, the team, my country, Regent Park. I wanted to score so badly, and I did. It's something that no one can take away from me, no matter what else happens."

The Russians allowed Krystal her moment before regrouping to score again, then again, winning the game 12–7. But after her penalty kick, Krystal kept coming and by game's end, she'd scored twice more—a hat trick—the first time a woman had achieved such a feat in HWC competition. The

Russians would march through the rest of the tournament, shredding other opponents before losing by a single goal to Afghanistan in the final. No team had scored as many goals against them as Canada, and no other player had beaten their goalie three times. Krystal was part of street soccer history now.

14

UP AND DOWN WITH THE USA

Having played six games over two days, which included a loss to Chile and a victory over East Timor, the Canadian players were now almost as battered as their replacement goalies. One of the players' amusements was to gather around Billy as he tensed his groin muscles, which sproinged like banjo strings as he pressed his legs together. "I have to sit in the shower for 40 minutes to get loose," he said, "and even then, I don't feel especially good. When you're tired, there's a lack of oxygen to the brain and you can't think right, you make poor decisions," he said. I told him that "Canadians Eliminated Because of Lack of Oxygen to the Brain" wouldn't make for the most sympathetic chapter heading, but he pfffted, telling me, "Hey, I can hardly get out of bed to pee. I just go to the window, hang it out, and shout, 'Look out below!' It hurts too much to walk down the hallway."

The rest of the team was in no better shape. Jerry's knees and ankles were killing him, and Krystal, despite her youth, was forced to apply bags of ice to her legs whenever she wasn't moving around. While Cristian maintained a coach's poise— the benefit of being 27 and not competing as a player—he was fighting insomnia and spent most of his nights wandering the streets and ending up in a downtown casino. Even Paul seemed wearied, burdened, as he was, by having to make sure his team stayed positive despite their disappointing results and the waves of pain that greeted them each day.

But if Team Canada was ground down by the vagaries of tournament play, it was nothing compared with what Team USA were going through. The Americans wanted badly to show well in the tournament, but they'd lost as many games as the Canadians had, and defeat seemed to sit less well with them. Dissent had also started to creep into their team, and the players groused about their playing time. It wasn't until the middle stages of the event that Tad saw much action, and because they'd ridden Tim as their number one goaltender, he was eventually knocked out of competition after myriad injuries. During a close, thrilling game against France, he'd leapt cross-crease to make a save but had rattled his skull against one of the goalposts, leaving him badly concussed and fighting a fever for the rest of the event. I saw him in his final appearance versus India, a dramatic game that both teams wanted desperately to win. The Indians showed a tremendous amount of fight against the larger Americans, drawing two yellow cards after heated altercations in the corner. In one emotional instance, Sawan, the once-lost Indian player, battled Tad, the reformed crystal-meth addict, for a ball along the boards. The players found themselves fighting shoulder to shoulder before the ball hopped into the court's green mesh. After watching it sail out of play, Tad extended his hand, and the Indian player responded in kind, as proud of their ability to play hard in the corner as they were of emerging from the encounter with their emotions in check.

While watching the Yanks play, I noticed one player— a Herculean African-American from Manhattan named Diego—reclining shirtless behind the team's bench. A former mortgage broker whose life mirrored the world's economic downturn, Diego had been recalcitrant throughout much of the tournament, complaining about his playing time and glowering during team functions. To his counsellor, he was still largely a mystery, even though he'd worked with him for the better part of a year. "He says that he's originally from Colombia," the counsellor told me, "but I'm not sure if he's being completely honest. He'd been doing some part-time construction work, but I don't know if there's drug abuse going on. I haven't actually gotten to the bottom of it. He told me that he never finished high school, but he went straight into selling junk mortgages, which shows a lot about who was lending. He has a South American pride thing and seems above reaching out for help. He lived in a shelter for awhile, but he still doesn't identify with being homeless. He's kind of reluctant to admit what's happened because it's impossible for him to swallow his pride. Admitting that he's homeless is to admit that he's a failure. The reason we brought him to Australia was because, during a team fight, he helped to break it up. He showed leadership, and we thought he'd be an asset. Still, I'm only now coming to the realization that he might just be kind of a dick. And when your homeless and you're a dick, life can be even more difficult and complicated."

If Diego's attitude grew more and more abrasive as the tournament progressed, his mood worsened after he received a distressing email from home. While he was away, a documentary about him had aired on YES Network, the New York Yankees all-sports TV station. The film showed Diego's fall from grace and his attempts to rebuild his life through the street soccer program. His estranged family saw the film and wrote to Diego, calling him a bum and a disgrace and telling him to stay away from them forever. To them, playing on Team USA only made him seem more of a loser than before. In their minds, being a private disgrace was one thing, but publicly admitting it was unacceptable.

If Diego was Team USA's burden, Juve was Team Canada's. He disappeared for days, limping in his knee brace across the city. He surfaced only occasionally to ask for spending money. When management asked Krystal if she knew what Juve was doing with his time, she reported, "He just walks around the city. I think he's meeting a lot of people. We stayed up all night and talked and after I got him to stop feeling so bad, I actually started to know him, inasmuch as anyone can know him." The coaches relayed this to the rest of the team, and Billy, in an attempt at being fatherly, offered: "Krystal likes Juve. It's obvious. But she's like a little lost puppy dog around him. I told her, 'It's not right. You should have more respect for yourself.'"

Because the team had no money, Paul reached into his pocket to provide for Juventus and the rest. He'd been doing this since he started the program, spending thousands to keep it going. He'd recently secured a grant of $80,000 from the Ontario Trillium Foundation in Toronto, but the money hadn't been released in time for the trip abroad. While other teams, such as the English, who are sponsored and mentored by Manchester United—their players train at Old Trafford before every HWC—and the Irish, who are bankrolled by the Federation of Irish Sports and cap their homeless players as true internationals, the Canadians have always struggled to find money to travel abroad. When I asked Paul why he continued to do what he did, considering the difficulties—financial and otherwise—in running the program, he recalled what had happened to his brother, a schizophrenic, and how it propelled him into a life of empathy.

"For years, my brother had undiagnosed schizophrenia. It was never properly dealt with. He had lots of jobs, but the paranoia would get too great, and he'd quit. He was an engineer, working for Husky and BMW, but his illness made it impossible for him to go forward. He got scholarships to Ohio and U of T, all that sort of stuff. My parents tried to help him, but things would inevitably end up in yelling and screaming fits. After he quit his last job, he started living in Bracebridge, north of Toronto, in cottage country. One night, he was driving back in his pickup truck when he skidded off the road. A helicopter came and brought him to Sunnybrook hospital in the city, and he ended up being in a coma. I was on a holiday with my first wife in Carolina at the time, and when I got the call, I came home immediately and went down to emergency. After two months, he eventually woke up. His brain was damaged, but strange things started to happen. For a week, he spoke French—we brought people to translate—and though the doctors said he wouldn't walk again, he was able to get to his feet. People at the hospital said they'd never seen such stubbornness in a patient, and to this day, they still keep in touch with each other. The irony is, this did nothing to cure his schizophrenia. But because he'd been getting such attention, he eventually met the right doctors and they were able to prescribe the right medication.

"After his rehab, I decided to take him in. I had very few options. My first wife and I had just bought a place, and so we renoed the basement. It was self-contained, but it meant that he wouldn't be on his own. It was a very stressful time. Because my brother was brain damaged and things weren't firing right for him, there were times when he'd become very angry. He'd berate us relentlessly, but a lot of the anger was directed towards my wife. I knew that she'd allowed him into our house because it's what I wanted to do, but she was never 100 percent behind it. It drove a wedge into our relationship, but I wasn't going to let my brother live on his own. My stubbornness eventually destroyed our marriage and my wife and I separated, then got divorced. Afterwards, my brother and I found ourselves in the same situation: alone.

"That spring, I felt the way a lot of people feel after their relationship fails. Not to compare my situation to what these players have gone through, but I don't think I would have started the homeless team if I hadn't been feeling as lonely and distraught after all of this went down. I started going to shelters with a soccer ball. I showed up and asked if anyone wanted to play. Inevitably, there were a handful of people, and we'd start a game. There was one player, Roger Friere, who lived at the Mavis Road shelter. He'd just gotten out of prison, but he liked to play, and it was good for him, just as it is for all of these guys. When you're alone, teams help you deal with that loneliness. You feel wanted, like you're part of something. Roger was part of the team that we sent to Stockholm. At the tournament, he met a woman named Elizabeth and fell in love. He made enough money to get back to Sweden, and they ended up getting married. Roger eventually moved there, and today they run the homeless soccer program together.

"When I first started doing my thing, it was in the suburbs of Toronto, but I hooked up with Rob at John Innes, and that's where the program really started to take off. My brother eventually moved out to his own place, too, and he moved to the city. The weird thing is, my brother lives only two blocks away from John Innes, on Richmond Street, and so do my parents, who moved downtown to be close to him. None of us can know where our paths will lead, but for some reason, a big part of my life has gathered around this section of the city. The players live and play there; my brother and parents live there. The way we got to this corner of the city might be different, but—homeless or otherwise—we're the same in more ways than we'll ever know."

15

THE WORLD
CUP FINAL
IN A TEACUP

THE MORNING AFTER the game versus Russia, I arrived early at Birrarung Marr for Team Canada's next fixture versus Mexico, the first match of the tournament's second stage, where teams were grouped together according to the results. Temperatures were already tickling the 30°C mark and the sun was grinning devilishly in the sky. On the court, the black turf would make playing conditions hotter still, and while circumstances were the same for both teams, the Mexicans had played in suffocating heat for most of their homeless-soccer lives.

Walking along the boulevard that morning, one moved upstream into homeless footballers and their fans shuttling from one game to the next. You could tell who'd won and who hadn't by the players' faces, and the most popular greeting was "How'd you do yesterday?" (The most popular response was, "Murdered Canada," but never mind.) The one team whose faces were unreadable, if only because they were always alight, were the small Filipinos, who moved about as if delighted by every detail of their visit. The previous day, they'd visited the Melbourne Zoo and were astonished by the penguins, whose movements they mimicked as they made their way to their first game of the day.

There was one player on the team, however, who appeared neither struck by the joy of being away nor particularly obsessed with penguins. I was told by the Philippines' manager, Antonio, who ran a 300-bed Catholic shelter out of which the homeless program was based, that the circumstances of the player's life had left him with permanent emotional bruises. He'd been abandoned early on by his parents, who'd left him responsible for his brothers and sisters. "The children were hungry and living on the brink of starvation before they found our centre," he said. "Because of the player's life, he never smiles. He is not capable of such expression, even though the rest of us are here, having the greatest of times. Oh, well," he sighed, with an air of resignation. "Maybe one day. Maybe."

FIFA chief Sepp Blatter had recently visited Antonio's centre after catching wind of the program's remarkable success in changing the lives of street kids from Manila and elsewhere. "I think he was impressed," said Antonio, "partly because soccer is not a big sport in Manila. It is basketball, which was brought to our country by the Americans. But because our church, Don Bosco, has roots in Italy, we were exposed to the game. I grew up playing with priests in their cassocks who taught me to love the sport. When some children come to us, they don't know anything about the game, but they learn soon enough. We had one girl who was incorrigible, who kept running away. But when she came back the last time, she started playing in earnest and now she is on the national under-19 team."

One of Antonio's players almost missed coming to Melbourne because he was unable to get the proper signatures for his passport. His father had died and his mother, whom the player hadn't seen in 10 years, had taken to scavenging as a way of supporting herself. "We tried looking everywhere for her," he said. "We had people roving the streets trying to find her, but when this failed, the government showed him some mercy and granted his passport anyway. Then, two weeks before we were supposed to leave, she appeared on our doorstep, and the mother and son were reunited. You can't imagine the tears, the emotion between them. But none of this could have been done without football—football!" he exhorted swishing his leg through the air.

Along the riverbank, the all-female Cameroon team— the Barefoot Engineers—had gathered at the embankment, where they weaved cornrows and braids for Aussie school children on a class trip, as well as for a few Red Cross volunteers. Cameroon's manager was a full-figured francophone woman dressed in a kerchief and matching gold and black robes named Giselle, who ran the street soccer program out of the capital city. Most of the women on the team were young, and almost all of them had young families back home. One of them was a 25-year-old mother of five who'd spent six months in India studying solar panel technology. It was the first time she'd left her village and the first time she'd been on a plane. Back at home, she was able to apply what she'd learned to the team's shelter, a mud brick structure that the players had built themselves.

Giselle told me a story she'd heard from a 20-year-old Liberian woman with an 11-year-old daughter fathered by a soldier who'd been offered the girl by her family as a reward. Giselle said that "life on the streets is very dangerous in Africa, more so if you're a female. A lot of women are abandoned by their partners, and unlike men—who shuck the responsibility of their families—women are obliged to take care of their children on the streets, too. It starts because many women are sexually uneducated and get pregnant far too early by reprobate men. For a long time in Cameroon, there was no place for these women—many of them travel to the city from the country—but we managed to mobilize our forces. We made all of the shelter's mud bricks ourselves and raised funds to build a roof and the doors. It's where we all live, together, protected from what, for many of our players, would be certain death at the hands of the streets. One of our players is lame, but we brought her anyway. You see her?" She pointed out one of the hairdressing players who'd coaxed another young Aussie girl to sit for her African makeover. "She sees that she can do this for people on the other side of the world, and when she returns home, she will maybe open a shop. This tournament isn't about winning, which is good because we haven't won much," she said, her great laugh echoing through the river valley. "Instead, it's about gaining real life-changing experience and feeling good about yourself."

Whenever the Federation Square stands were full for important games, it was like watching the World Cup final in a teacup. At full capacity, the park could barely contain the press of spectators jammed shoulder to shoulder on the makeshift stands and surrounding piazza, which shook with sound and colour. The loudest and most colourful of these fans were the Afghanis, most of them young, earringed refugees with frost-tipped hair waving enormous red-and-black flags and hand-painted signs. They arrived early for their team's games to sing Afghani pop songs and soccer hymns as a way of ramping up the enthusiasm until the moment their countrymen hit the court. It was only calm at the end of matches, when the Afghan team fell to their knees in the middle of the court and starfished in prayer before rising to continue what would be their inexorable march to the tournament final. They'd leave the park to find their supporters waiting for them, and, behind them, a tangle of young Australian protesters carrying STOP THE WAR IN AFGHANISTAN! signs and placards, forgoing any of the fans' joyful toasting.

The boys from Kabul were young and terrifically fast. After watching them throughout the week, rival coaches and players agreed that they were, in essence, the heart of what would have been the country's under-20 national side, had such a team existed in their war-ravaged home. Their entry in the tournament, in fact, stretched the notion of what constituted a homeless team, raising the question of whether being displaced by war properly qualified them to play against men and women who largely dwelled in the streets. The Afghani coach himself hinted at this during a midday press conference, suggesting to Mel Young through an interpreter that he change the name of the tournament. "In Afghanistan," he said, "there is really no such thing as homelessness. If you do not have shelter, people will take you in, no matter what. If we win this trophy, we will be hard pressed to parade it through the streets. Homelessness represents something far worse in our country than in other places. To be homeless in Afghanistan is to be considered deranged or infirm. It represents a lowly condition that is shunned by a lot of our people."

There were suspicions among some managers that the Afghanis, being as fit and wildly skilled as they were, were using the tournament as a way of showcasing their skills for potential employment on one of the many Aussie pro sides. This suspicion was partly confirmed when it was revealed that, two years before, the Afghanis' sponsors had built a four-on-four pitch, where they trained every day in hopes of prevailing as champions.

The play of the Afghanis—and the Scots, Irish, Kenyans, and Russians, too—was street soccer at its finest. It was certainly more kinetic than many other 21st-century sporting aberrations, like air racing or televised tournament poker. Played on a tiny court, it dispensed with a lot of the traditional game's midfield and defensive tedium, which, in North America at least, has prevented a lot of people from embracing the sport. I thought it was an ideal game to be sandwiched onto a television screen. Sadly, local or international media didn't share this view. The only televised tournament game was the event's final, which was aired on one of the local cable access stations. And local beat writers stayed away in droves, reporting only on the event's opening day and its conclusion. Even then, most of the stories were about the teams who'd sought asylum, and questions about whether or not burdening the public with these defections justified staging the event at all.

One of the challenges of the HWC's organizing committee was to convince disbelieving writers and other sportsmen that, even though their athletes were homeless, they played a game high in skill and drama. This cynicism was expressed by a reporter who told me that "When I first raised the idea of covering the tournament to my editors, they said, 'The Homeless World Cup? What kind of events do they compete in? Dumpster diving? Panhandling?'" For many, the event had to be seen to be believed, but without any kind of mass media coverage, its reach would only extend as far as those who saw the games first-hand.

It was a shame, for instance, that only a few thousand witnessed a semifinal game that pitted the Scots against the English. For two halves—14 minutes in total—the ball never stopped moving about the field, a hot potato that required players to move fast to gain control and think fast when dispersing it to an open player. Street soccer was like a windup version of the traditional game, and if purists were loath to embrace a torrent of goal scoring over technical acuity, I wondered how they would have felt had they watched the Scottish and the English storm each other's goals, drawing gasps from a crowd reluctant to miss a second of play. After the game moved to a shootout—the losing team would be eliminated from the event—it was so silent that it was as if someone had pressed a pillow over the crowd. When the Scottish prevailed, they were swallowed by a roaring group of fans, as well as the entire Irish homeless team, who burst onto the court, consuming their brothers in green and white. And when the final produced the dramatic and politically charged matchup that pitted the Russians against the Afghanis, you could see what the HWC had over other soccer competitions, creating new dance partners and giving an opportunity to troubled countries that might not otherwise have found a stage.

There was more than just a continental tie that bound the Canadian and Mexican sides. Mexico's coach was a gentle-voiced psychologist named Daniel Copto who'd lived in Toronto before returning to Mexico City. He'd also been involved in helping set up the program at John Innes, even before Paul and Cristian had come along.

"I grew up in Mexico City," he told me one afternoon at the university. "I was the second oldest of four boys. Everyone went to university, and I studied to be a psychologist. One of my brothers ended up moving to Toronto, and I followed him. It was very tough going in Canada. In 1995, I had to work my way up from the bottom. I worked at Pizza Pizza as a driver, earning five dollars an hour, even though I had my psychologist's degree. Those people who show up at your door with your pizza? That was me. I was over-educated and working a menial job.

"After a while, I became the superintendent of a building and a waiter for a catering company, always holding down two jobs. It was rough and I was beaten down by the end. Because I hadn't used my knowledge of psychology, I almost stopped believing that I had it. When you're forced to do things you don't really want to do, you start wondering who you are and what you're doing. You get swallowed by your efforts to merely survive. I'm not saying that I was on the streets myself, but if I hadn't worked hard and found these jobs, who knows? Despair and a feeling of defeat can come to anyone, quickly, like this," he said, snapping his fingers.

"I ended up going back to school, Durham College, to study addiction counselling. I had friends who had trouble with alcohol and drugs. They'd come to me for advice, and I'd tell them where to go. I didn't counsel them, not officially, but they knew that I had a natural way of dealing with these problems. After graduating, I found work at a local mission. I tried to be helpful without expecting anything in return. The biggest challenge was to walk into a setting with all of these

English-speaking people. They were distrustful of me at first because of my accent, and there was a certain amount of prejudice because I wasn't from Canada. But I learned how to get close to them. I was relentless and don't tire easily.

"There was one fellow who was schizophrenic. He came every day to the mission. One day, he was just walking around the dining room. He was in a fantasy world talking to an imaginary friend, whom, I learned, was the president of Brazil. One day, I decided to walk with him, saying nothing in the beginning. He allowed me to walk alongside him, so, slowly, I tried to become part of the conversation, talking to the president, asking him things to keep the conversation going. One night, I asked this person if he would let me take him to the hospital, and he said yes. He ended up staying there for months. His doctors had had trouble getting through to him, so I helped out. Everybody was amazed that he would talk to me but no one else. Eventually, he left the hospital, never to return. Then, years later, he showed up at the mission, perfectly healthy and sane. He was a complete and functioning member of society."

"I started to work at the Good Shepherd shelter, across from John Innes. There was one fellow, a crack addict, who'd been in and out of homes, the whole bit. We became friends and I asked if he wanted to play sports. I went over to John Innes and organized these sessions, just playing games, nothing serious. It seemed to work, at least for him, and he got clean. I knew then that there was something there, that sports could work as a way to rehabilitate people with problems."

Perhaps it was because of the teams' natural bond that the Mexico-Canada match yielded little in drama or intrigue, or, to the Canadians' chagrin, closeness of score. In the end, the Mexicans defeated Canada easily, but the game would be remembered not so much for the score but for what happened afterwards. As time elapsed, both teams came together along the centre line, their arms wrapped around each other, waving to the crowd. Watching this from the crowd, Tim, the USA goalie, told me: "I was of half a mind to run out there, too. One big stinkin' continent standing together on a soccer field."

Canada would barely have time to catch their breath before playing Namibia, but if the players allowed themselves a spare moment to regenerate—more often than not, this involved stuffing themselves with packets of Starburst provided on endless flats in the dining lounge—the team's management would have no such reprieve. It was discovered that, after playing Mexico, Ned, the goaltender, had disappeared. Paul asked the Australian reserve coach to find him, but he was told that Ned had contracted the flu and wouldn't be playing. In the end, they produced a young Kiwi goaltender named Tim, who had an Air Jordan logo tattooed on his calf and who'd just been released from prison for crimes related to heroin abuse. When Billy heard the news about Ned's disappearance, he wasn't surprised.

"When we first met him, he was bouncing around, shouting, waving his arms. It was great, right? Right," he said, raising his eyebrows. "He was using, man."

"How did you know?" I asked him.

"How did I know? I'll tell you. Yesterday, Jerry and I were walking back to our dorm when we heard this awful sound. We looked through a bunch of bushes and saw Ned, dry-heaving over and over again. I'll tell you one thing: you don't get the dry heaves when you have the flu. He's going through withdrawal, man. He's got it bad."

I deferred to Billy in these matters. "It takes a user to know a user," he told me. "Once you start reading the signs, it's easy to see."

One evening while nursing a pint at a nearby pub, Billy walked into the room, sat down, and took in the scene at a glance. "That guy there," he said, pointing to a fat man in a floral shirt with a woman sitting on his lap. "That guy is the dealer. The girl sitting with him buys drugs from him. Maybe she gets them for free, if you know what I mean," he said, poking me with his elbow. "Those other guys over there," he continued, gesturing at two high-strung men who were involved in a loud, relentless conversation, "are users, too." I called him on this last observation, but, moments later, the two men disappeared into an alley and returned to their table high-fiving and sweating.

"It's the way it works, man," he said. "I've been there. You go to a bar. You're with your friends and you do some coke, whatever. Then you make friends with the guy who sells you the coke. The next thing you know, you're going back there more and more often. And the next thing after that, you're sitting in the back of the bar, stoned, where nobody but the dealer can find you."

Cristian said: "In the beginning, I was the same as you. I couldn't see it the first few times, but you start to notice things: the eyes, the mouth, the posturing. I knew immediately when we left John Innes that Eric was high."

"Something to remember," said Billy, "is that 50 percent of what a user tells you is bullshit. They don't even see you. Mostly, he's just thinking about where his next score's gonna come from, even when he's high. You think I talk a lot now? But before, look out."

Over the final few days of the tournament, I saw Ned once, maybe twice. I approached him one day in the stands, but it was all he could do to look at me, peering through faded eyes and tightening his jaw as he spoke. Before, he'd been a font of energy, laughing and joking with the players, but now he was gravely anti-social. One night in the players' lounge at the university, he stopped to wish Billy good luck in the rest of the tournament, the pouch of his hoodie weighted with soda-pop bottles he'd taken from catering. "Can't decide what to drink, might as well take them all," I joked, pointing at the pouch. "Yeah, I got 'em all," said Ned. After he left, Billy told me, "He's going to drink all of those at once to try and get a sugar high. Poor guy's trying to do everything he can. I hope he makes it, but it's the toughest thing a person can do. Going cold turkey is like getting stabbed in the neck with steak knives. I don't think it helps him that he lives where he lives, with drugs all around him. Triggers, man. You've got to get rid of the triggers."

By the end of the tournament, Ned was AWOL. He was lost to the streets before a champion was crowned.

16

WHEN
YOU'RE
TOO TIRED
TO RUN

Moments before the start of Canada's next game versus Namibia, Vannie reappeared along the bench. The team was delighted to see him and took his presence as a positive sign. But Vannie hadn't shown up to support the team. Instead, he said to Paul and Cris, "I should play for you. Not him." He pointed at the Kiwi, Tim, who was warming up in goal. "I win for you. It's true, no? I win." Paul and Cris told him that he was right and that they'd try to get him for one of their upcoming games. It was more words than any of us had heard Vannie speak at a single time. After he left, Cristian said to me, "Man, what a chatterbox. Couldn't get him to shut the fuck up."

As the teams finished their warm-up, I visited the announcer's booth in an effort to get them to play a Canadian song during the team's introduction. They handed me a ringed binder, and I rifled through the pages, hoping to find "Canadian Railroad Trilogy" or "Snowbird" or "Blow at High Dough." There were only two CanRock entries: Steppenwolf's "Born to Be Wild" and Bryan Adams's "Summer of '69." I said that these would do in a pinch, but instead the Canadians were introduced to "I'm Gonna Be (500 Miles)" by The Proclaimers. Perhaps Krystal had gotten to them first.

I also asked the announcers if they wouldn't mind using the players' nicknames when calling the game. They were more than willing to do this. When I canvassed the team about what they wanted to be called, Jerry and Krystal said that it didn't matter, but Billy said, "Call me 'Ironhorse.' You know, like Beckenbauer, Platini, Maldini, all of the old ironhorses, because that's what I am." I set off to inform the announcers, but Billy called me back. "Or 'Van Damme,'" he said. "Yeah. Tell 'em to call me 'Van Damme.'"

The Namibians wore silver and blue, while the Canadians were dressed in white shirts and red shorts. Both teams had similar records—a few key wins and twice as many losses— but it was hard to know what to expect from the game. After the referee rolled the ball into play, it seemed as though neither team wanted it. But it was Krystal who seized the ball first, controlling it for a moment before sending it crosscourt to Van Damme, who was standing near the boards and, I thought, leaning against them. After taking a long exasperated look at the distance required to run upcourt, he swung his leg backwards and hammered the ball at the Namibian goalkeeper, a tall, sinewy woman with a severe limp in her right leg. As the ball climbed into the air towards her, she put up her hands like a person surprised by a large barking dog. The ball found the green netting behind her, making it 1–0 for Canada. Afterwards, Van Damme explained his shot, saying: "When you're too tired to run, you just shoot."

Quickly, the score became 3–0. This was both the best and worst development for the Canadians, for it tricked them into thinking that they didn't have to run too much. It also played to their goodwill nature, their desire not to show up the young Africans, something that Cristian had drummed into them before the game. But the Namibians—who were half the Canadians' average age—recognized their opponents' fatigue and quickened the game's pace, eventually putting five goals past Tim, who appeared bewildered by the assault. "No fucking way," said Billy, wiping his brow. Jerry shook his head like a man trying to wake himself up. The only player who absorbed Namibia's sudden burst of life was Krystal, and it was she who worked to pull the game back in Canada's favour.

With the score narrowed to 5–4 for Namibia, Krystal was awarded a penalty kick. As she'd done against the Russians, she touched her crest twice and kissed her hand before rolling the ball forward and burying the equalizer past the Namibian goalie. She scored the next goal, too, but the Africans tied the game soon after, then went ahead with only a handful of seconds left to play.

It was all the Canadians could do to will the ball downfield. After gaining the offensive zone, Jerry, his great belly swinging in repose, held the ball under his foot in the corner of the pitch and appeared lost in thought, perhaps wondering whether or not he'd turned off the stove before leaving for Australia or, more likely, imagining what a small hockey puck would look like at the end of a dildo. A Namibian defender leapt from his position to try and wrench the ball free, but as he did, Jerry flicked the ball at the net, squeezing it past the surprised African goalkeeper.

Time lapsed and the game was pushed to a shootout, the first of the tournament for Team Canada. It was almost too hard to watch the ending of the match. Cristian announced that Jerry would take the team's first, and possibly only, free kick (shootouts were decided in sudden death). Even though Krystal had beaten the goalie twice and Billy had taken hundreds of successful penalty kicks during his life, Cristian wanted to spread around responsibility for the game in an effort to reinforce the notion of team, perhaps even at the expense of a victory. To Cristian, the event was about sharing effort and learning from competition, even if it meant eschewing traditional sporting wisdom.

As the referee called Jerry to the court, the schoolchildren who'd marched with Team Canada in the parade reprised their "Ca-na-da" chant from the stands, and it was to the tweeness of their voices that Jerry walked towards the ball. He moved slowly from the centre line, juked one way, then another, then fired the ball—*whoam!*—only to hear the defeated clunk of the metal goal frame rattling after impact. Jerry groaned, threw up his arms, then let them fall to his sides in anguish.

The Namibians shot next and Tim hardly moved. The ball sailed into the mesh, and the game was over. From the sidelines, Jerry turned to me and joked, "Not scoring on a girl with one leg. Put that in your book." His response made it seem as if Cristian's idea of play and his choice to let Jerry shoot was probably the right one. But as I turned around, Billy gestured for me to lean in to hear what he had to say. "I was the one who should have shot first, not Jerry," he grumbled, his face pinched in disappointment as he stalked off the court.

17

FUCKED

UP

WE ALL HAVE parents, some good, some not so good. In most cases, parents try to do right by their children, raising them to be decent citizens with a strong moral centre and the ability to judge good from bad. The rest of it we fuck up ourselves.

The only parents who'd come to watch their children play in Melbourne were those whose sons and daughters played for the Australian men's team or their female counterparts, the Street Matildas, a thrown-together side who'd been assembled only a day before the tournament. A woman named Toni, who'd previously played on the men's homeless team, captained them. She told me that, after leaving home at 15 and taking to the streets, the situation with her parents was steadier than it had ever been. But one afternoon in Federation Square, I saw her and her mother embroiled in a long argument. Toni stabbed a finger at her mother and yelled incomprehensibly. The mother folded her arms, a wan smile drawn across her face. Toni threw out her arms and yelled, "Fuck you!" The mother turned her head and looked into the distance. Toni stormed away.

Another of the Aussie parents was a woman named Susan. Her daughter, Michelle, was among the most unlikely players in competition, having battled heroin addiction, bipolar disorder, and cervical cancer, which she'd developed as a 28-year-old prostitute. On occasion, I noticed her sitting by herself with her head in her hands, her long stringy hair draped over her face and shoulders, looking up only to pull from a cigarette stuck between her fingers.

When I asked Susan how she dealt with having an addict as a child, she laughed at the apparent absurdity of my question, saying, "She's 31 years old! She's not a child anymore. She's her own person with her own life." I tried not to show her that I found her answer cold, because it was obvious that she had deeper and more complicated feelings, which, after a while, she began to explain to me.

"My daughter became addicted to heroin when she was 15," she said. "At the time, she was living with her father, who gave her a lot more slack. For some unknown reason, she didn't want anything to do with me. I think it was because her dad worked for IBM, had a great income, and did everything that family law court tells you not to do when you separate: buying her expensive jeans, and all of that. He tried to pull the reins in, but it was too late. I've tried every which way to help her, but she's very stubborn and single-minded. As a kid, I'd catch her drinking and tell her not to, but it didn't do a lot of good. The resentment only grew between us to the point that she totally shut me out. But I've got my son, whom I live with. At least he's doing well," she said, sighing.

"I'm over it now because it's been going on for 16 years," she said. "It never really leaves you, but I've learned to deal with it. I tend to not let things get to me like I used to. As a mother, you do everything you can. You nurture them, put them into sports, point them in a healthy direction. But," she said, folding her arms, "it's not really in my control anymore. Maybe it was at one time, but it's hard to measure what's already been done. I used to count the scars, but not anymore. They're too many to number, really."

One afternoon, I found Michelle attending a symposium that included representatives from the African women's teams. I told her that I'd spoken to her mother, and wanted to ask her about some of the things she'd told me. She said, "Yeah. Okay. That'll be fine, I guess," so we wandered into the sunlight, where she sat smoking and talked about her tormented life.

"I get along a lot better with my mom now. I'm aware of all the shit that I did and I feel sorry for her that she had to deal with it. I know that I put her through hell and back. As a kid, she put me in AFL [Australian Football League] little league and I played on a team called the Demons of Melbourne when I was seven or eight. I had big opportunities when I was younger but the dope got in the way. I was supposed to play softball for Melbourne—they were gearing me towards playing for the national team, as well—but I got into pot and it snuffed everything out. I was a bit of a wild child. I didn't mean to be, but I had a very rebellious streak. My mom was so anti-everything. She was very strict, and I didn't speak to her for eight years. She dressed me until I was 12 years old, which was when things started to change. I wanted to break loose, but she couldn't embrace it then, and she can't embrace it now. But at least we're talking, and, you know, that's a huge step forward in our relationship.

"Looking back, my parents separating had more of an effect on me than I realized at the time. My dad still smokes bongs on the weekend or every second weeknight, and back then, it just seemed normal. My mom would get really stressed out and she'd not only take it out on me, but herself, too. She probably didn't tell you, but she attempted suicide a few times. She just couldn't handle it. But now, instead of asking me why I am the way I am, she says, 'Oh well, Michelle, that's just you being you.' It's better. It's a start.

"After I started smoking pot, I got into amphetamines," she said, "and then heroin. Some people think that smoking pot's okay; some don't. It's different for everyone. Heroin ended up giving me extra confidence, but before I knew it, I was working on the streets to maintain my habit. It happens to a lot of girls, from families good and bad, rich and poor. Ninety percent of the girls working down at St. Kilda are on heroin. It was a good life for a while. I lived like a queen, making a thousand dollars a night, done by 11 PM, going home to a decent flat. I had a shit lifestyle, but at the end of the day I had everything that I wanted. The drugs helped numb all the crap and bullshit that you have to go through. But things started to change for working girls once the cars got central locking. Men would lock you in so you couldn't get out, things like that. Sometimes, they'd rape you, or get physical. The wintertime was hard, too, standing out there in your skimpy top. Half of the girls would get the flu or really bad colds. I had a chronic flu one time, standing in the rain with my broken umbrella. Another time, I was using at the top of a staircase when the cops showed up. I couldn't get my gear away fast enough, so they threw me down the stairs, where they kicked and spat on me. The cops are a lot better now. They've learned to accept that prostitution isn't going to go away, but, in a way, things are also a lot worse. Younger kids are getting into it, 12 and 13 years old. There's a place in Sydney called "The Wall" where 10-year-old boys are out there selling their bodies. I worked in Sydney for a while, at Kings Cross. It's always been a lot heavier up there, 300 girls a night, and lots of violence, people getting murdered.

"I eventually started dealing heroin, but, one year, seven people OD'd off my stuff. I started to feel like a murderer, but there was nothing I could do. It was an epidemic. Still, I'd had enough of the life. I got so frustrated with the scene, working night and day and never having time for myself, so I tried to detox. I've been off it for two and a half years now and I'm on the methadone program. I started taking 160 milligrams a day, but now I just need 25 mills. I hope to get off it, eventually. That's my goal anyway."

When I asked Michelle to explain what the tournament had meant to her, her answer was different from anyone else's. Pausing to consider her words, she said, "I don't get very mushy about things. People can say how they feel all deep and meaningful about it, but to me it's just another event in my life. I don't know. Maybe not until it's over will I realize what it meant, but I don't ever really appreciate things when they're happening. I don't respect or understand them until they're finally gone. That's my life, you know," she said, taking a long drag on her cigarette, "and that's how I've fucked it up."

$=18=$

KRYSTAL
AND THE
CAMBODIANS

WHEN OTHER MANAGERS talked about Team Canada, they talked about one player: Krystal. She was easily the most prolific female scorer in the tournament, had played almost every minute of every game, and was among the event's leaders in goals, the rest of whom were men. Before Canada's game against Cambodia, Paul and Cristian were approached by the Dutch coach, a fellow named Steven Coleman, who had competed internationally for Holland and who ran a women's soccer program in Rotterdam. Not wanting to get anybody's hopes too high, he told them that there were scholarships available and that he could probably use someone like Krystal on his side, provided he could convince his superiors that saving a spot for an international player would improve their team.

Paul and Cristian told Krystal nothing until they knew for sure. It would only hurt her if the offer turned out be premature. Still, they were thrilled that a tangible opportunity might come out of the event. That Krystal had left such an impression while playing below her athletic capacity—she'd only just started playing again, and because she smoked cigarettes and pot, her fitness wasn't where it had to be—supported the case for Paul and Cris's program as a kind of soccer hothouse for the downtrodden. But Cristian was also clear about his team's goals. "If she gets an opportunity to play in Europe because of this: great. If she doesn't: great," he said. "Krystal and all of the players have carried themselves with a lot of dignity and spirit, and, in the end, I hope they feel better about themselves afterwards."

The dignity and spirit of the Canadians was in evidence against Cambodia. The youngest player on the Cambodian team was 11; the oldest, 22. They wore dark blue and white uniforms and looked like a peewee team when standing in the shadows of the rangy Poles or the Ghanaian giants. No men's team at the HWC had played less football in their lives than the Cambodians, three of whom were born in the dumps of Phnom Penh and still lived there. While other teams had found it difficult to raise funds and draw players into their programs, few teams' journey to Melbourne had been as emotionally fraught as that of the Cambodians, having left three players behind at the airport on the day of their flight.

These circumstances were explained to me by a young Irishman from Tipperary named Paraic (pronounced "Poric") Grogan, whose job it was to help coordinate the team's entry into the tournament. His NGO worked with Cambodian groups helping children born into abysmal poverty, many of whom, he said, were sold into brothels. They had given local groups the responsibility of assembling the team. From their end, they arranged flights and gathered the necessary paper-work. It was also Paraic's job to get the team to Melbourne and to see them through their experience in Australia.

When Paraic showed up at the airport on the day of their departure, he discovered that three of the players—who'd arrived for their flights with their extended families in tow—had been placed on the team by government officials trad-ing favours with well-to-do local citizens. Unlike the rest of the team, none of the boys were homeless. Paraic cancelled their tickets on the spot and told them to go home. Despite a dramatic and troubling scene at the airport terminal, Paraic stuck to his guns, feeling that the whole spirit of homeless soccer had been blighted. He also knew that including the sheltered, well-to-do boys on the team would jeopardize sub-sequent visits to the tournament.

"Our coach, who's with us now, argued with me to bring them, but I felt that it wasn't fair," said Paraic, who seemed distressed while describing the experience. "I haven't told him yet, but there's no way we'll bring him again. I'll let him enjoy his time here, but he gave me no support at all. It's a real issue in Cambodia, having foreigners work in sporting programs over there, because any success you have results in Cambodians feeling bad about themselves, knowing that one of their own wasn't able to achieve success. Something simi-lar happened to a Kiwi who was coaching their rugby side after they won a few games abroad. It seems as if the Cam-bodians would rather be a captain of their own sinking ship rather than a passenger on one that's sailing ahead."

Although the economy in Cambodia had improved by eight percent over the last few years, things were still very bad throughout much of the country. People who live in the garbage dumps range in age from four to 40, and their life-span is twenty years less than the Cambodians average, which is 56. They work sorting through garbage, living on 25 cents a day by selling whatever refuse they can find.

"One in fifty Cambodian adults has AIDS," Paraic continued, "and there's a huge slave labour issue, with children being sold into brothels. One woman I knew said that she'd rather die of AIDS today than die of starvation tomorrow. It's sad because, before the Vietnam War, Cambodia was, in many ways, a model economy. In 1956, the Singapore government had actually travelled to Phnom Penh to learn how to build a proper South Asian economy, but these days, the Cambodians look to them for help. The education system is corrupt and teachers won't teach unless they're bribed by the students, who have to pay them something extra before every class. This is a direct result of the Khmer Rouge, who imprisoned or killed every intellectual and educator in the country. But because there's relative peace now in Cambodia, there's a feeling of guarded optimism in certain corners, though the truth of the matter is that it will take an enormous effort to rise above the conditions that afflict most of the people. The kids who live in the dumps live in the worst situation imaginable. Their only way out, in a lot of cases, is to join the local gangs, who traffic in glue. One of the first things the gangs do is get poor children who are eight, nine, or 10 years old addicted to the stuff. By the time they're teenagers, they're mentally damaged and all they know is glue. But because it's the only thing that helps them escape, the gangs have them for life."

Because of Paraic's decision to hold back the domiciled players, he understood that "when I return to Phnom Penh, which I do two or three times a year, there are parts of the city

I can't go to. I have to worry about my security. If I find myself in the wrong part of town, I'll likely get jumped and suffer the beating of my life, maybe worse."

Those Cambodians who managed to get to Melbourne possessed something that many of their countrymen lacked: a passport. "It's a hugely significant piece of paper," said Paraic. "It will help them if they want to pursue any kind of education. It will help them if they want to go by bus to Thailand or Vietnam, and if the economy somehow improves, they can work for a company where travel is required. It gives them immediate status and recognition and is a huge advantage as a way of potentially improving their lives. If they've had any impact at this tournament at all, it hasn't come from their games—all of which we've lost—but from the fact that other athletes have heard what they've gone through. When you hear about someone who's had to live in a dump or been sold as a slave to a brothel, you realize that your own life, however fucked up, isn't so bad after all."

I reported the story of the Cambodians to the players before the game, and while they would have reacted the same way without this information, it was all Billy and Jerry could do not to roll them the ball on a velvet runner. At one point, Billy gave the ball to the goalie after he'd errantly dropped it out of his crease, at which point the announcer exclaimed: "That's what the spirit of the Homeless World Cup is all about, folks." The players let the Cambodians dribble up court and shoot unchallenged and offered them the ball when offside or out-of-bounds calls went against them. Because the game was an easy win for Canada, Cristian and Paul spent most of the match with their eyes trained on Steven Coleman, the Dutch coach, who watched from the sidelines along with one of his dreadlocked players. There wasn't much that Krystal could show in battle worn skills versus Cambodia, but the coach was looking for other things, anyway: first and second touches, a nose for the net, defensive capabilities, and speed. But these skills had been displayed elsewhere, so there wasn't much more that they needed to know. After the two teams congratulated each other at game's end, Paul pulled Krystal aside and told her that the Dutch national coach wanted to talk to her.

There was a meeting behind the pitch, a few feet from the riverbank. Coleman spelled out his program, and Krystal listened. Though she'd been a quivering arrow of life all tournament, she was now still, carefully leaning in to hear the coach's words. "I can't promise you anything," said Coleman, holding up a hand. "Nothing. Not now." Then he turned to Paul: "Can you get me all of her information: where she'd played and at what level?" The manager said that he could get it to him by the morning. Before the Dutch coach left, he smiled and told Krystal, "You have a good left foot." She thanked him, speaking for the first time.

After the coach left, Krystal turned from the group and walked to the riverbank, her eyes downcast. She found one of the young Cambodians sitting alone and sat beside him on the embankment, leaning her elbows on her knees and putting her chin in her hands. Then she rubbed her face, and looked away. Her teammates moved to congratulate her, then stopped. Krystal shook her head slightly as if trying to make sense of what the coach had said. She turned and said something to the Cambodian player, but he held out his hands, not knowing what to say. She smiled and patted him on the shoulder, and he nodded and smiled back.

= 19 =

THE

WANDERER

T HE LAST DAY of the tournament centred on the event's six finals, in which the advancing teams were graded according to their results. The Canadians earned enough points to make it to the lowest group final—Group D—where they would play for the International Network of Street Papers (INSP) Networking Trophy. While a second victory over Cambodia had proven decisive, the players weren't kidding each other. They'd survived to play another day because the Swedes and Belgians were also part of their group, and it was impossible not to do better than them. Still, even though they'd backdoored their way into the final, Team Canada relished the opportunity to bring home a trophy.

Because of the importance of the final games, I decided to put away my notepad. As the game approached, the players grew serious, training their thoughts on what lay ahead. Because they didn't have much time left in Australia, it was essential that they enjoy what was left of the experience. Having someone with a pencil and a tape recorder probing them with personal questions was the last thing they needed.

Juve returned for the final day. When I asked what he'd been doing with his time, I was surprised when he suggested that we sit and talk while the rest of the team prepared for their important match.

During his time alone in Melbourne, Juve had hit the streets. It was no big deal, he said, having wandered for most of his life. "I know how to meet people, how to talk to them. And by 'them,' I mean women. You have this cast on your leg and if you walk around with a good attitude, it's easy," he said, lighting a cigarette.

"I met a lot of women. A lot," he said, boastfully. "You see, I like women with big asses. It's my thing, you know." He held his hands in front of him as if groping an imaginary cushion. "One day, I was standing in front of the train station. This one woman was looking at me. I looked at her, she looked back, and she smiled. She had a nice ass, a big ass. Anyway, we started talking a little bit and made plans to meet. We went for dinner, a very good meal. I met her friends, then more friends. We had a party. We went to some bars. It was great. Then she took me home. This happened once, then twice, and then it happened again with another woman. Me, I've had a good time here, even with this stupid injury," he said, tapping his knee.

"I met other people, too. I like this city. It is not like Canada. It is open and free, and people will talk to you. It's like London, where my brother lives. It makes me think that maybe I will go there and see him and be with him. Maybe it's time for a change, eh?"

This was the first time Juve had mentioned his family, but when I asked him what his brother did and where he lived in London, he refused to answer. "I can't talk about that. There are things I can't tell you for my safety, and for your safety, too, my friend," he said, touching my arm.

"I took trains," he continued. "I went out into the country, moved all around. I found the Moroccans. I went looking for them. I asked people and found a restaurant. They were good to me, gave me a great meal, introduced me to their family, everyone. This is the Moroccan way, the African way. We look out for each other, you know?

"Then I followed them to a hall, a theatre in a school, and there was a Christmas pageant going on. I didn't really understand it, but I sat and I watched. It was good," he said, shrugging his shoulders. "It was strange because it was about Christmas, but, you know, they were nice people. I liked them. Then we went back to the restaurant. And that's when they told me to stay." He tapped his cigarette ash to the ground.

"Meeting those people showed me something. It reminded me that, in this world, you can go anywhere. It is up to the individual how he wants to live his life. Everything in life comes down to the individual and the choices you make. I will be all right. I will be okay."

"So you're not staying?" I asked.

"I thought about it very seriously," he said. "If I stayed here, I could have a good job. I could have a really nice girlfriend. It would be a good life, believe me. But Paul and everyone else— Cristian and Keith—it would be wrong for me to leave them and walk away. It would be very complicated for them."

Even though he'd only played a minute of soccer, I suggested that maybe, in his own way, Juve had learned something while at the Homeless World Cup.

"A team is still a team no matter what. You don't turn your back on your players and coaches. And don't forget it: I am part of this team."

After talking to Juve, I joined the team along the riverbank, where Cristian was readying them for a pre-game talk. Billy came up to me and said, "What did Juve tell you?"

"He told me that he liked women with big asses."

"Yeah, you know why?" he pfffted with an air of indignation.

"Why?"

"Because they're easy to get into bed, that's why."

I SAT WITH the Canadians in silence along the riverbank before their final game. At one point, a yellow bird perched on a bench, chirruped, then flew away. "You know, in Greece, if a bird visits you, it means good luck," Billy said.

"Any bird? Even an Australian one?" I asked.

"Especially an Australian one," he said.

Canada would play Malawi in the final. Their record was almost identical to Canada's. "We can beat Malawi," said Jerry, rubbing his hands together. It was the first time anyone had mentioned winning since the early days in St. Kilda. The notion was just as improbable as before. By tournament's end, Team Canada's players looked the way Pommie did when we'd first met him: half-broken and fatigued, bandaged and bound in gauze. At Cristian's insistence, Billy had visited the medical tent and was diagnosed with a strained ligament in his knee. He walked in a painful pigeon-toe, grimacing with every step, and the doctors expressed surprise that both of his ankles had remained fused to the bone. Jerry's knee also required the kind of prolonged rest that the tournament couldn't provide, and, at one point, he borrowed an American player's set of crutches and duped an organizer into driving him back to the university. Still, because they'd booked a ticket to the final, they were determined to play, and play hard, provided they could walk.

Cristian gathered the players together in a huddle and said: "Winning doesn't matter right now because, in a way, you've all won. You're champions to me and to Paul, no matter what. We might not be among the best teams in terms of wins and losses, but we're the best in the sense of what the Homeless World Cup represents. You came here as a four-person team, and then you were three, but you embraced every player who joined us. You made them feel welcome, and that's huge. You played honest, friendly, and competitive football against all of our opponents, and you showed every one of them equal measures of respect. We haven't had a single penalty card drawn against us all tournament, and that's also huge. You've treated wins and losses the same, mixed well with other teams, and you've gone out to see as many games as possible. You're exactly the way Canada likes to think of itself in the world and exactly the way it should be. I can't say enough, guys, really, I can't. Now go and beat the crap out of Malawi."

If the Homeless World Cup was undoubtedly, indisputably, based on the notion of goodwill and humanity and sharing one's experiences with others, it was also about sport, and since sport is largely about winning, it's what the Homeless World Cup was about on its final day. After Cristian had finished, the players sat unmoving as they waited to be called to the field. They seemed frozen by the weight of the moment: chins steady, eyes boring into the distance, shoulders braced for their moment of sporting truth. Just then, one of the tournament's liaisons came bobbing through the boulevard's mass of fans. Shuffling alongside him, holding a Brazilian pennant in one hand and a lunch bag in the other and looking like a young boy lost at a carnival was the person who would play goal for the biggest game of Team Canada's homeless soccer life. "I've got your star goaltender, fellows," announced the liaison.

Vannie.

THE CANADIANS followed their goaltender to a spot behind the bleachers of Federation Square. Vannie sat down on a set of stairs and trembled. It would be the first, and only, game he'd play on the main field, and the look on his face suggested dread and terror. "Look at poor Vannie. He's shaking," said Billy. As the frail, jittering goaltender struggled to put on his shin guards, Cristian noticed that his knee straps had come unhinged, so he knelt in front of Vannie and helped him snap them in place, as if he were dressing a small child for his first game.

The Malawian team arrived and gathered next to the Canadians. While their respective coaches made small talk and wished each other good luck, the athletes kept their distance. Malawi's only female player stared at Krystal as if trying to drive nails into her soul. Billy laughed and said: "Hey, Krystal, someone over their wants to be your friend," gesturing with his head at the player. Krystal raised her ever-present headphones from her ears and said, "What?"

"The girl over there. I think she likes you!"

Krystal looked over, and the player tightened her menacing glare.

"Oh, hey, hi," she said, returning to her iPod and dancing lightly on her feet.

When the teams were announced, they jogged together up the stairs to the field. The day was warm and sunny, and the soft black rubber of the pitch was warm to the touch. Balls sailed around the court as the two teams warmed up, while the crowd murmured expectantly. "Here we go!" shouted Paul, as if at the crest of a rollercoaster ride. "Dave—Eric's gloves!" shouted Krystal from the field, and so, one last time, I tapped the players for good luck before returning to the bench.

The Malawians had one very good player, but only one. Still, because he was half the age of Billy and Jerry, he hadn't suffered the kind of wear and tear that had worn down one-third of the Canadian team. When I asked Paul whether he'd requested Vannie for the game, he said that it hadn't been his idea. But when the organizers looked at the list of teams competing in the final, it didn't take long for them to know which team would best accommodate him. Trophy or no trophy, Canada had embraced whomever had joined them, and, they were as excited to have Vannie behind them as they would have had Gianluigi Buffon strolled down from the stands.

Well, maybe not quite.

Moments before the referee rolled the ball into play, the court was stilled, and both teams stood quietly in position like infantrymen listening for the first rumble of an assault from above. Then, as the ball left the referee's hands, the two teams lunged after it in a ragged chorus line of ankles, feet, and toes. Suddenly, the announcer cried, "And Van Damme has the ball!" Rising to the early drama of the game, Billy pushed a gust of air from his cheeks and blasted a shot at the Malawian goal. The crowd drew in its breath as the ball took flight, then exhaled as it sailed ten feet above the court.

"Okay, okay," said Billy, calming himself.

Billy's shot was a portent of things to come. One could only wonder what might have happened had his shot seared into the back of the net. The Malawians fired a long shot of their own, and Vannie played it like a person trying to trap a mosquito between his hands. This was followed by another African goal, and then another, and while the Canadians answered, the first half ended with Malawi 7, Canada 3.

Then, as the second half began, something remarkable happened: Vannie started stopping the ball. It's impossible to say how he did it or where he'd found the concentration required to hold the Malawians at bay, but, suddenly, he was saving the ball, even if he looked like someone falling off the back of a boat or getting shocked with a cattle prod while doing so. The announcer told the crowd that Vannie was a member of the Aussie reserves, and before long they started a great roaring chant—"Vannie! Vannie! Vannie!"—which the Canadian coaches fattened from the bench.

The Canadians scored twice more, but the game ended 12–5 for Malawi. For the players, the 14-minute game must have passed in the flick of an eyelid. "Well, we tried," said Jerry, wiping his face as he came off the field. "We did our best out there." Billy added, "It's over; it's finished. We don't have to play anymore." If being sore and physically taxed had an upside, it was that it masked whatever hurt the players might have been feeling in their hearts. At the game's end, Krystal stared dejectedly at the field, rolling the whys and what-ifs over in her mind. She couldn't have seen it herself, but even in defeat, Canada's homeless soccer team had achieved something significant. Leaning on the boards drained of energy, they looked like any other team at any other tournament, and if the results of Paul and Cristian's homeless soccer program were hard to quantify, here, the effect was obvious. They looked normal.

NO
DIRECTION
HOME

AFTER THE GAME, Paul told the players not to leave. After a few more divisional finals, they were going to get their medals presented to them on the field. Billy harrumphed: "I've gotta go back out there? Man, I just want to sit and watch the games."

"C'mon, Billy, it's a medal. Your medal," said Paul.

"Medal? I've got a whole shelf of medals back home," he said, groaning while limping towards a seat in the bleachers.

A little past midday, the players were asked to assemble behind the pitch. Organizers cleared the field after Zimbabwe defeated France, transforming it into a presentation stage with lecterns and microphones and a table arrayed with hardware. The city's mayor and a few local councilmen were produced, bringing with them a phalanx of security personnel to herd the teams who'd played in the finals and escort them out for their medal ceremonies. The scene behind the pitch tightened a little. The crowd seemed confused and a little exasperated that play was suspended to accommodate the midday pageantry. "Too many suits," Paul whispered to me as the Group D finalists were called to the field.

As the players walked out, the game's score was posted on the Jumbotron in glittering script. Paul and Cristian thought it was callous, and Jerry did, too. "Like I need any more reminding," he said, peering over his shoulder. The announcer said: "With their 12–5 win over Canada, let's hear it for the winning team from Malawi!" The crowd cheered and the Canadian players' hearts sank, just a little. We stood on the field and watched as the Malawians received their trophy.

A local dignitary carrying a silver tray with medals for both teams lassoed the Africans with their gold discs. Then he walked past the Canadians and placed the tray back on its table. And then the Canadians were called off the field. There was a moment of confusion as security led them to the sidelines. "Wait, this isn't right," said Paul. He turned to the security person and said, "Those are our medals. We're supposed to get them."

"What's happening?" asked Krystal.

"We're going the wrong way!" said Cristian.

"Just keep moving, sir," said the security guard.

The Canadian coaches tried fighting their way back to the field, but they were blocked, and before they knew it, they were behind the pitch, without medals and angry. Krystal pushed her face into her hands and ran away. She'd wanted the medal to show to her nephews. It wasn't a big deal to her, but it was a big deal to them. "But there we were," sighed Billy at the end of the day, "Shagging the pooch in front of 8,000 people."

Paul was appalled by what had happened and assailed one of the organizers, who was full of regret but said that because the rest of the presentation was underway, it would be impossible to bring the team back on to the field. He was at a loss what to do but promised, "We'll make it up to you. I promise we will. I promise."

Still, it wasn't good enough. After all that the players had been through, Paul felt as if they'd been shafted. As we climbed into the stands to watch the final games, he shouted to anyone who would listen: "So this is how the players are treated?" He almost immediately regretted his outburst, but his emotions were understandable. While players get to work out their frustrations on the field, coaches and managers have no similar outlet. It was hard enough to hold a team together, let alone hold it together himself, and after all they'd been through trying to assemble the team—finding the money for plane tickets, wrangling unresponsive local team chapters, fixing it with their employees to be granted time off, and making sure the team's experience at the event went as smoothly as possible—you'd excused Paul if he'd thrown the shit-fit to end all shit-fits right there in the middle of the coronation. Instead, he went looking for Krystal, who was hanging with the English, who were commiserating with her. After he returned to the stands to watch Afghanistan defeat Russia 5–4, I suggested to the coaches that, after all they'd been through, they probably owed themselves some patio time. They agreed. We found a pub near Federation Square. The waitress brought us a sweating tray of Blondes and we murdered them.

Afterwards, Paul and Cris headed back to the dorm. I remained downtown, not quite wanting to let the tournament go. Before joining the team for the awards ceremony at the university, I wandered into a small pub across from the train station. There was music playing at one end of the room—a grey-bearded and pot-bellied local pickup band. Two of the musicians, it turned out, were lorry drivers; another was a postal worker; another tended bar at another pub. If they'd traded their instruments for soccer outfits, you wouldn't have been able to tell them from the players, which says something about how close the musician—and artist, generally—is to the bottom of society. The band's repertoire consisted mostly of covers by the likes of Badfinger and T. Rex, with "Hey Jude" and "Revolution" thrown in. While the musicians played, their faces were pressed with the kind of satisfaction that comes whenever people with shitty day jobs find themselves freed from the worries and tensions of life once they grab their instruments and turn them up loud. Although they had homes, jobs, and possibly families, the effect of music on them wasn't so different from what sport meant to the athletes of the HWC. The small crowd afforded the group mostly cheerless applause, but nevertheless they leaned into every song, wrenching every last bit of release that their playing provided.

The final song of their set was "Like a Rolling Stone" by Bob Dylan. Like all musicians, Bob Dylan had been down there, too, riding with the hobos, playing for the tramps. From the first clack of the drummer's sticks, the singer keened into the song, chewing through Dylan's lyrics about the nature of the streets, which, both on the recorded version of the song and this one, belied the band's buoyant rhythms of hope. The crowd listened and swayed to the melody as emotion tightened in my throat. The singer sang *how does it feeeeel?* He sang about being on your own, a complete unknown. He was singing about himself as well as the soccer players, who were packing up and leaving the park en masse. The singer howled through the chorus: *to be on your own!* A few people sitting along the bar raised beer glasses and sang along: *like a complete unknown!* I thought that if anything came of this crazy soccer tournament, maybe the homeless players would have less reason to feel alone, and that, one day, they would be unknown no longer.

THE AWARDS CEREMONY was staged under blinking purple-and-red lights and a disco ball that twirled during the post-ceremony celebrations. It was a final chance for players to see each other before they returned home. A Brazilian player named Carlos was named tournament MVP, and when his name was announced, his teammates carried him to the stage, his feet dragging against the ground, hands flattened over his face as he wept openly with joy and surprise. The Team Canada players, as well as many of their competitors, were almost certain that Krystal would be named the tournament's Best Female Player. But the award was given to a Liberian woman, Dehkontee Sayon, who wore green HWC shoelaces tied into her ponytail and who could barely walk to the stage after suffering an ankle injury a few days before. After her name was announced, there were few cheers among her teammates, and I wondered what she'd done to have been received so coldly by them. As it turned out, only one of her teammates, captain Bendu Goi, attended the ceremony. The rest had defected that morning, leaving the two players and a cobbled together lineup of Australian reserves to play the victorious Zambians in the final. While the Canadians were disappointed not to see Krystal recognized in front of the others, there was no begrudging the Liberian woman. That she'd chosen to return to her country showed courage worth rewarding, and while leaving one's African home for a chance in the developed world was no less valorous, damned if the Homeless World Cup was going to hand out an award for that.

The last token of the night went to the Afghanis for winning the tournament. Speaking for his players, the team's manager reminded the crowd that his country had been at war for 35 years and that the players had trained amid threats of suicide bombers and other hair-trigger violence. "I cannot leave this stage without informing you," he said, soberly, "that today, nine more people—our neighbours, our brothers, our mothers, and our children—died in a gunfire attack in our home in Kabul. This is what we suffer through every day. This is our fate and this is our life." Then he tucked the award under his arm, descended the stage, and vanished into the crowd. This was the last anyone would hear from either him or his team. Like the Liberians and the players from Zimbabwe, the Afghanis would also seek asylum in Australia, their play for freedom splashed across the headlines of the morning's papers. The citizens of Melbourne would read not about the tournament's record-setting attendance or the personal triumphs of Tad or Krystal or Arkady or P.J. or Dove or the Belgians or the team from Sierra Leone, but about how the Afghanis had arrived under the pretence of being soccer competitors, but, in the end, merely thickened the ranks of Australia's dispossessed. In most reports, event organizers were quoted as saying that, as a result, the Afghanis, Liberians, and Zimbabweans would be banned from subsequent tournaments. "What they've done," one source told me, "has damaged our reputation. It makes it very difficult to stage this tournament at our whim, wherever we want to take it."

The celebration appeared to have ended as the gathering of players and management—including Allesandro, who'd shown up in a beautiful beige suit, which he'd hauled all the way from Milan—turned away from the stage. But it became apparent that there was still one more award to be presented. A silver-haired man in an expensive suit—a local member of parliament, it turned out—stood at the microphone, tapped it twice, cleared his throat, then announced, "Before we finish here, we have one more trophy to present. This trophy is perhaps the most important one of the evening. It embodies all of the things that the Homeless World Cup stands for and it is about playing with honour, determination, and great spirit. It is the Fair Play Award, and this year it goes to..."

"Canada!"

Krystal bolted into the air, her small fists punching skyward. Billy turned to Paul and Cris, his mouth hanging open as if to say, "We won an award?!" Jerry and Juve hugged, and Paul and Cris took turns slapping each other on the back. Bewildered and delighted, the players made their way to the stage, running a gauntlet of arms and hands lashing out at them in affection. They stood before the crowd holding an engraved silver plate exultantly above their heads as the chant of "Ca-na-da!" was sounded one final time. Watching from the back of the room, I was struck by the poignancy of the moment. Billy had come to the award after losing his restaurant and the trust of his parents before rising above his addiction; Krystal had dealt with the loss of her mother and an aimless, unhappy teenagehood to play the game she was born to play; and 20 years ago, Jerry had fought his way back from dissolution after his wife had given birth to twin girls before leaving them a few months after her delivery. For years, he'd worked shitty jobs to support them as a single dad, suspending his dreams of novelty dildos and space-age seat cushions to the point that, once the girls were old enough to go to school, he was left with nothing, so he headed to Calgary, where he slept on couches and in shelters trying to realize his vision, only to see it squashed by nefarious and greedy lawyers distrusting of his ability to see his dream through. It wasn't until months after the team returned to Canada that he told me this. Even so, he asked if I would give him a new name and distort his portrait so that his girls wouldn't find out what had happened. I told him that I'd do what I could, and when I sent him this text to look over, he said he'd get some notes to me after he returned from a Palm Springs' trade show. Turned out he'd won back his patent and had been able to take on an employee: Juve, whom he'd invited to stay in his small apartment, where he was expected to recover fully from his injury.

When the awards ceremony ended, we adjourned to Billy's room. He'd decorated it fine, with soccer posters and beer mats and some red-and-white piping he'd found on the university grounds. Paul hauled in a box of 48 beers, but everyone was too tired to drink. Jerry sat in the corner exhausted and spent, so it was left to Krystal to shit-talk her teammates, making fun of Billy's shotmaking and Jerry's age. Her face was like a glowing lantern in the dim light of the room.

"You talk that way in the Netherlands and Coach Coleman will have your ass," said Cristian. Krystal, reminded of her

European opportunity, buried her face in her hands, halfway between laughing and crying.

After a while, we dragged ourselves back for one last encounter with the other teams at the courtyard, but there wasn't much left to say. The next day, the players turned together and faced a single direction, heading to a place that was now something to return to, instead of somewhere to leave.

Home.

EXTRA

TIME

ALMOST IMMEDIATELY after Melbourne, the John Innes homeless soccer program expanded tenfold. This was partly because of the large grant that Paul and Cristian received from Trillium and partly because everyone was energized by the experience. A few weeks before I finished this book, Cristian reported that participants in their twice-a-week games now numbered in the hundreds, and, according to his math, the program had positively affected about 97 men and women. One of the first things they'd done upon arriving back in Canada was keep as much of the team together as possible, entering them in men's indoor soccer leagues, Billy and Krystal running the offense while, Eric, if still burdened by his habit, tended goal. The team had gone to the finals twice only to lose in extra time. On a few occasions, however, their efforts made the front page of local papers and, at this writing, they were poised to win the division of a new league, where better and more experienced teams were among the competition.

I followed the 2009 team to Milan for the next year's HWC, where the experience was almost opposite that of Melbourne. Regretfully, the Italians—whose organizing committee was run by Allesandro and Bogdan—housed all players miles out of the city centre in army barracks, their grounds patrolled day and night by soldiers and policemen. After a few days, Paul moved his team to a hotel in the city—burning his budget for the sake of showing his players at least a semblance of Italian city culture—but this only partly made up for the fact that the games were poorly attended and, because the teams were distanced by location from each other, the comradery seen in Oz was hard to find.

Still, Canada had a terrific tournament, owing, in part, to its youth, and the fact that Daniel Copto had lent them two young Mexicans for most of the games. One evening, after a full day of matches, I'd arranged for the team to dine at a restaurant called L'Ulmet, in one of the city's oldest, narrow corridors. The osteria had been recommended by a friend, and it wasn't until we showed up wearing our soccer warmup jackets and shorts that I saw that the restaurant was more than we'd bargained for. L'Ulmet ("fig leaf" in Italian) required that patrons buzz themselves in, providing the maître d' approved of one's comportment. Looking through the window at the dining room's antique flowered urns and fine white tablecloths, I feared the worst as its proprietor, a Borat-esque young man in a beautiful suit named Manolo, approached the door.

He peered through the curtain and greeted us. He looked over the players and management and I was certain we'd end up back at the McDonald's that sat at the end of our street. But after I told Manolo that my friend had suggested that we visit his place, he whisked us inside. People turned to stare at us as we stood in the entranceway in our ragged red-and-white outfits. He brought us to a table and handed us menus and, after we'd finished the finest and most delicious of Italian meals, he brought the players down to the restaurant's 15-century wine cellar, where he poured grappa and asked them about their lives. Afterwards, Ritchie Reynolds, a fortysomething player who'd battled depression after being abandoned by his parents, expressed his wonder at the evening's events. "I usually go to the food bank," he told us. "I eat whatever they put in my bag, but this evening—and that food—I'll never forget, no matter what."

BEFORE GOING TO Milan, Billy and Eric had come to visit the 2009 edition of Homeless Team Canada. Billy stood before them as someone whose life had found its axis after he got involved in street soccer. In the span of six months after Melbourne, he'd reconciled with his parents, secured his own apartment, and was helping to manage an equipment manufacturer, Anaria, with whom Paul and Cristian and others had a relationship (Anaria had previously donated gear to the team). "I just wanted to say to you guys," he told the team, "that you can do anything you want to do on the field over there [in Milan]. And whatever happens, it's just a start. Respect the game, and it'll respect you. And if you respect yourself and you're right in the head, anything—*anything*—is possible," he said, pointing at the players.

Krystal hadn't come to John Innes, and she hadn't played a lot in the homeless team's most recent indoor schedule, but there was good reason for this. Arriving home from Melbourne, she was disappointed—everyone was disappointed— to discover that the Dutch coach had neither the tenure nor the authority to pick and choose who came to his program in Rotterdam: he had spoken out of turn. But, in the end, it didn't matter. With Cristian's encouragement, Krystal had tried out for Toronto's best semi-pro women's team, and made it. On weekends she travelled around the province with her new teammates, scratching out homework on the bus, before getting a call that every young female soccer player dreams of: Team Canada, under 19. If she made it, she'd become the second Canadian to play for both the national homeless team and the national team, proper. Billy, of course, was the other. While the team managers were loath to admit it for fear of jinxing their progress, an athletic pattern seemed to be emerging.

Despite their progress, Paul and Cristian kept a lid on their enthusiasm, stressing that the program wasn't about athletic advancement or winning or losing. But neither of them could have imagined how their program would affect these men and women, how playing a simple game would inform their sense of destiny and self-worth. They hadn't reinvented soccer, but the success of the Canadian homeless soccer program was theirs. For that, they owed themselves a few Blondes, and, one hoped, a moment or two of contentment.

DONATIONS to Street Soccer Canada can be made by going to canadahelps.org and typing in "street soccer canada," or by contacting the author at hockeytrope@hotmail.com.

Donations to Street Soccer USA can be made by going to streetsoccerusa.org and clicking on "Get Involved" or by emailing event@streetsoccerUSA.org.